To Andrew.
with Love
from
Auntie Dot

. . . for the riggings were of thread, and the perfectly shaped
yards were no thicker than match sticks.

THE HOUSE OF GOLDEN WINDOWS

Adventure Story for Children
9-11 years of age

By

A. HARCOURT BURRAGE

RYLEE REWARDS
RYLEE LTD. LONDON & BIRMINGHAM

Printed in England
by
LOVE & MALCOMSON, LTD.
London and Redhill

CONTENTS

CHAPTER I

MYSTERY HOUSE

WHEN the Strathmore children first arrived at Syre, with brother Noel's school friend Malcolm Brewster, they had eyes for nothing in particular but for everything in general, until the evening. They stood in the garden of the house Mr. Strathmore had taken for the holidays, which was on the west cliff.

Even the tide was soundless in the golden light of sunset, and the gulls white-speckled the rugged cliffs that had for ages defied the Atlantic.

Malcolm Brewster and Noel Strathmore had climbed

into the branches of a gnarled and tempest-bent tree on the very edge of the cliff, but Gwen would not permit her young brother, Dudley, to run such a risk. The two elder boys were showing off, and Gwen was suitably impressed.

" The House of Golden Windows ! " suddenly exclaimed Dudley, breathlessly, just as though he had discovered an enchanted palace.

None answered immediately. They stared across the hollow between the mighty cliffs, wherein lay snuggled the little village of Syre, with its toy harbour and small fishing fleet, and such white cottages on either side of the steep and cobbled street.

There was a high wall all round *the house* that stood alone on the rugged heights. The massive and rusting iron gates were closed and looked as if they were never opened. It was a house of mystery, and very little was known about those who lived there. Indeed, none of the local fisherfolk could have told anyone even the name of the person who owned *the house*.

" Someone lives there. I can see an open window," shouted Malcolm, from his vantage point in the tree.

In silence, they continued to stare at the House of Golden Windows. The windows were like eyes of burnished gold winking and flashing in the glare of the setting sun.

It seemed to Noel and Malcolm that all kinds of mysteries might be found in that house, and to Gwen and her younger brother it was really a dwelling in a fairy story.

The glare of the gilded windows made the high wall, and the ivy that climbed to the very chimney-stacks, look very dark.

Gradually, the windows lost their fire and loveliness, and became " like eyes of a dead fish ", then *the house* looked particularly evil.

Mrs. Spraggart came trotting from the house in which their father was writing a book, with their mother helping, to call her " chicks " to bed. If she had worn feathers instead of a neat print dress and a snow-white apron, they would have been ruffled like those of an angry hen. She was once their nurse, and now the house-keeper. Although Mrs. Spraggart ruled everyone, and always seemed to be in an " awful state ", as she called it, she was lovable and much loved by the Strathmore family.

" You two kids had better go to bed," ordered Noel, catching sight of Mrs. S.

Gwen and Dudley ran down the twisting path and into the house, followed by the plump Mrs. Spraggart, whose round face looked as if she had polished it with furniture polish.

There was no further need to " show off before the kids ", so Malcolm dropped to the ground, and Noel joined him. They wore only shorts, and the visitor— who had naturally assumed command of the Strathmore children and had already decided that they should pre-tend to be Devon Smugglers—had sketched the skull and cross-bones on his chest in burnt cork. Noel hadn't liked to say that smugglers did not wear the skull and cross-bones.

"I'm going to find out all I can about that house!" Malcolm declared. He had dark curls and flashing eyes.

"You bet we are," agreed Noel, pulling his wooden sword from his belt, as though every cabbage in the vegetable garden, through which they passed to the drive that ran steeply down to the cobbled road, hid a Preventive man.

"Leave weapons at home," ordered Malcolm, with a secretive air. "We mustn't arouse suspicion tonight. We're peaceful citizens, spying out the land."

Noel felt that he had sadly erred in having withdrawn his sword, but quite reasonably protested in a spirit of self-defence : "Anyway, Clever, what about your skull and cross-bones?"

Malcolm licked his handkerchief and rubbed off the gruesome design, smearing the tan of his chest with traces of burnt cork.

They had a good hour before they need go to bed.

It was dusky and very still down at the cove. The shadows were long and dark, and everything looked unreal and mysterious. The pale light slowly faded, deepening and enlarging the shadows until objects melted into "nothingless" as Dudley once said of a late twilight hour.

The harbour wall was forsaken. There was no one about, and not even a light gleamed from a window of a cottage. It almost seemed that the folks of Syre had met somewhere in secret, as once the shipwreckers of that evil coast foregathered to plan destruction to some gallant ship.

Fishing nets were spread to dry along one side of the cobbled road close to the harbour arm. The few fishing boats hugged the harbour wall. There was a faint smell of dead fish, seaweed and tar.

The two chums sat on the harbour wall, eyeing " The House of Golden Windows ", now a frail shadow against the deepening sky.

" People who shut themselves away always have a secret, Noel," whispered Malcolm, taking it for granted that someone lived in the house. " Or there may be a prisoner there. With that high wall and those covered iron gates, the place seems more a prison than a home."

" Rather, and anyway, who would want to live there unless they were made to ? " asked Noel.

" Yes," agreed Malcolm Brewster. " And I'm jolly well going to find out who lives there. Who knows, it may be some poor captive in need of help. I bet the local people are afraid of that house and won't talk about it."

Noel nodded.

He, too, had read stories about lonely houses on bleak cliffs.

Some houses do look as though they keep dark secrets

from the world, and that was how Noel and Malcolm felt about that house.

Suddenly, Noel turned his head and stared up the cobbled street, that was steep and narrow. He was alarmed to find that a tall, broad-shouldered man stood close behind them. He was dressed in a blue jersey and serge trousers very wide at the bottom. Sailor's trousers. His feet were naked, and his features were tanned the colour of walnut juice.

His teeth were vivid white as he smiled upon them in a friendly manner.

" Oh . . . Hullo," said Malcolm, and then added in his surprise, in a breathless whisper : " 'Ware spy ! "

" Good evening. You boys arrived today ? "

The man's features were strong and rough ; the face of one who had weathered many a storm. His hair, of short, tight curls, was raven black. His keen eyes, his bold chin, and the general massiveness of his build reminded both boys of pictures of a buccaneer. Indeed, had the stranger worn gold ear-rings, a colourful shirt open down the front, and a broad belt stuffed with pistols and a sword, they would have regarded him with no more awe and wonderment.

But there was something friendly about his smile and the expression of his eyes. They did not feel afraid of him after the first startle of surprise. He lit a cigarette and lounged against the wall, and began to ask all kinds of questions until he had learned all about them, but he said nothing about himself beyond the fact that he lived alone in a nearby cottage, through the open door of which they saw the glow of a bright fire.

" If it's boating you've a fancy for," he told them, " I'll run you boys out for the asking."

" We've got a boat," answered Malcolm, feeling it was time he took the lead again. " At least, Mr. Strathmore is going to buy one."

" Well, then you can ask me to go out with you," laughed the stranger. " There's swimming, fishing, boxing and making model ships if you ever feel that way. I'll be glad of a little company now and again. The local folk don't take kindly to strangers. My name's Spanyard."

The two young friends introduced themselves belatedly and separately. Then a brief silence followed.

Malcolm Brewster—as self-appointed leader—felt that caution was necessary. He thought Noel was far too friendly towards the stranger.

" Tell me," asked Malcolm, glancing towards the lonely house on the east cliff, " who lives there ? "

Mr. Spanyard's smile thinned : " There's not much known about who lives there. If I were you boys, I wouldn't ask or try to find out."

With which remark, he strolled towards his cottage in the dusky background, and closed the door.

The rebuff—although perhaps the stranger had had no intention of behaving so strangely and in a manner so unfriendly—swept a vivid flush to Malcolm's cheeks.

He stood, proud and defiant, watching Mr. Spanyard's retreat, feeling that he had been told to mind his own business.

" Perhaps we'd better be getting home," suggested Noel, feeling a little angry towards the stranger. " I say, before the door was closed did you see a model of a ship ? I do hope Mr. Spanyard will teach us how to make one, don't you ? " he asked, eagerly.

Malcolm Brewster did not answer. He thought he was clever enough to " draw an honest fisherman ", for such Mr. Spanyard appeared to be. His speech, however, was that of an educated man.

" Rather ! " he answered, without giving thought to his chum's remark. " I say, it may pay us to keep in with him. I believe he knows something about that house ! "

The stranger had made a deep impression upon the two boys.

" I don't believe you like him, Malcolm," Noel whispered, conspiratorially. " But I do . . . rather. I think we ought to make a friend of him. He might be able to tell us all kinds of exciting stories. Anyway, father may not let us go sailing alone and he's no time to spare, having to finish his book."

" If Mr. Spanyard knows anything about that house," boasted Malcolm, having decided there was a mystery, " I'll get the story out of him. I don't think I altogether trust him ! "

They strolled up the cobbled street in silence and had almost reached the end of where the nets were drying when a man stepped from the shadows.

" I couldn't help overhearing your remarks ! "

He spoke pleasantly, and smiled in a friendly manner He was thin and tall, and foreign-looking. A pointed beard and a neatly trimmed moustache and a sallow complexion gave him a foreign-looking appearance. He was handsome and dignified. His eyes were keen and not altogether kindly, but shrewd to the extent of being perhaps cunning. In a strong light, those eyes would have looked like jet marbles.

" Sorry I've startled you," he added, suavely. " I was enjoying a quiet smoke. On an evening so still even a whisper travels. I couldn't help overhearing. I do hope we will become friends, for I like you both. I'm staying in the neighbourhood. I am interested in history and buildings."

" Oh, it doesn't matter in the least, sir, that you overheard us," answered Noel, thinking how like a French Count the stranger looked.

" You've made friends already ! "

" We don't know that gentleman who spoke to us, sir," answered Noel.

" Neither is he a native," grinned the stranger. " Curious, what he can find here to interest him. Well, well, I'm just as curious about that lonely house as you two splendid boys. I get lots of fun out of being curious.

That house on the cliff, I'm sure, has a mystery. That man who spoke to you may tell you something, when you get to know him better. I'll be coming back soon. We'll meet again. Good-night."

The stranger strode away, taking a sharp bend and disappearing. A moment later the chums found him standing by a powerful car that had not been there when they had come down to the harbour earlier.

" You must wonder why I'm curious," he remarked. " Two intelligent boys might even be suspicious. I'm writing articles for a newspaper on ' Strange Homes and Houses '. And sometimes I write the history of places I visit. Interesting, eh ? Good-night ! "

He entered the car, waved his long, white hand, and drove away.

In silence, Noel and Malcolm climbed the rise, passing a few white cottages. Here and there a light now gleamed, and the rugged cliffs looked ghost-like against the night sky. Above, a few stars shone.

The incoming tide now and again muttered and splashed amid the boulders.

Syre seemed a very mysterious and secretive place that first night of their holiday.

CHAPTER II

THE LONE WATCHER

NEXT morning, Mrs. Spraggart told her " chicks " that she did not wish to be fussed and bothered by them during the day. She spoke her mind so crossly that one might have thought they were a great trial to her, instead of being the joy of her life.

Mr. and Mrs. Strathmore had already settled down to their new masterpiece—which Mrs. Strathmore declared was really her work, laughing gaily as she said it—but they would play smugglers after tea, or play anything else the young tyrants demanded of them.

The dark-haired, reckless Malcolm Brewster was gentle

and considerate in the presence of Mrs. Spraggart, and not a little afraid of her. But he greatly respected her for the dear old body she was.

Mrs. Spraggart had lunch packed for her " chicks " in a huge basket. They were supposed to be smugglers and, as such, could not be seen with a basket. She found some linen bags in which she repacked the " contraband ", arguing all the while that she had never been a smuggler, but if she had been she would have used a basket.

She watched the young rascals depart, smiling all over her huge, happy face, and waving as though they were off for goodness alone knew how long.

Mrs. Spraggart was certain that one at least would return with a torn garment, and all would be in need of a bath.

" The work they make ! " she anticipated, delightedly. " Wears a poor body to the bone."

She saw in Master Malcolm the leader of much innocent mischief, and liked him for his frank, strong spirit, the ease with which he assumed leadership over Master Noel.

Doubtless, she thought, Master Dudley would rather have remained alone with his books and dreams, but had shouldered his contraband, and had followed Gwen without a murmur of protest.

A day in the open would do him much more good.

Malcolm declared, as they slipped wooden swords into

their belts and tied colourful handkerchiefs around their heads, it would be safer if they set out one by one and met " at the spot when the moon was low ".

" The spot ", was close to the House of Golden Windows on the east cliff.

Malcolm outlined orders, as they arrayed themselves in the summer-house on the edge of the cliff.

There could not possibly be a smuggler's band without an oath and rite of membership. Each would have to be known by a special name.

Before any of the others could as much as " hoorah ", Malcolm said he would give details later.

Then they set off.

Gwen went first with Dudley, having been carefully instructed as to the secret paths they were to take.

None thought of sending Dudley on his own. He looked too small and frail to be a " lone hunter ", so Gwen, as usual, looked after him.

Gwen had fixed brass curtain rings to her ears, and wore wellington boots, to the tops of which had been sewn gaudy frills.

The boys were barefooted.

No sooner had the first pair set out than the elder boys stripped to the waist, used burnt cork with which Malcolm Brewster sketched a skull and cross-bones on his chest.

Noel preferred a sailing ship.

It must be remembered that smugglers, pirates, and

such desperate rascals have a choice taste in tattooing.

By time the two friends were decorated, they were due to set off upon their dangerous adventure.

Because of their contraband, they did a great deal of crawling, dashing breathlessly from bush to bush. They finally joined their equally daring companions in the shade of some bushes, close to the wall surrounding *the house* on the east cliff.

The top of the cliff was green, sloping away to a misty valley landward, that was dotted here and there with orse in full bloom. The sea was blue and, far below, the wave-crests looked like feathers floating shoreward.

The harbour and the few fishing-boats, and such cottages as could be seen from the height, looked toy-like.

Dudley, seeing how like real smugglers Noel and Malcolm looked with their tattooing, opened his shirt and borrowed the piece of burnt cork. He asked Gwen to give him a " fierce moustache ".

The contraband was hidden beneath the bushes nearby.

Their thoughts were turned towards an old wooden door in the wall. It was a door, of rough, heavy wood, looked as though it had not been opened for centuries.

Above the old wall, that was very thick, could be seen some of the upper windows of *the house*, and the tops of storm-distorted trees. Gnarled branches bent over the wall as though a fierce and silent storm forced their limbs to lean in one direction.

" The swearing-in ceremony can wait," suggested

Malcolm. " Let's find out what is on the other side of the wall."

" Oh, Malcolm ! " protested Gwen, for a moment forgetting that she was a desperate smuggler lass. " Wouldn't that be a very rude thing to do ? "

" Avast, traitress," retorted the bold Malcolm, showing his teeth in a snarl of contempt. Then he added in a somewhat calmer mood : " I shall be able to see over the wall where its broken away. That is, if I stand on Noel's back. I don't mean to trespass, silly."

" It looks awfully high," remarked Dudley, having already smudged his " fierce moustache ", for the satisfaction of twisting its ends. " And suppose you are seen ? "

" You kids," commanded Malcolm, grandly, " will take the contraband fifty leagues to the sou'-west, and there hide it until the main strength joins you. We can afford to run no risk. 'Ware Preventive men or disaster may befall you."

He waved his sword towards some gorse bushes about fifty yards away.

" The password is ' pancake ' and countersign ' jam '," he hissed, as Gwen pulled the contraband from beneath a nearby bush, taking the heavier load herself.

" Keep to the secret trail, my worthy men," warned Malcolm, which reminded Gwen and Dudley that they were supposed to dodge and creep between the bushes, and crawl across the open, ears and eyes alert for the presence of the vigilant and dreaded Preventive men.

It was only a few yards to the wall, but Malcolm chose to crawl round several bushes in the wrong direction before he made for the foot of the wall.

Close to the wall, the stinging nettles were thick and very painful. Both regretted they had left their shoes and stockings at home.

"Listen, comrade, mount the fastest steed you can place hand upon, and bring back Gwen's footwear. Hasten, for the moon is not yet up and there is time if you haste. Our fate is in your hands. Good luck!"

Malcolm shook Noel by the hand, and frowningly watched him "ride through the night to the thunder of hooves upon the frosty air". That meant, in plain language, running to where Gwen and Dudley were watching from behind some bushes.

He borrowed his sister's wellington boots and, after some galloping in and out of scattered bushes, set out on a direct course for his valiant leader.

Malcolm Brewster waited with arms folded across his chest, feet planted firmly apart. He glared defiantly at the wall.

The boots proved to be too small for Noel, and he suffered not a little agony as he walked amid the nettles, with his friend upon his back.

"Press your head against the wall and don't bend too low," whispered Malcolm. "Keep steady while I climb upon your back. I don't want to land in the nettles."

Noel dutifully obeyed. Malcolm stood on his bent back, gripping the top of the wall. He was just able to peep over the top.

"See anything?" asked Noel, scratching a sting on his right knee.

Malcolm did not answer.

He was seeing a great deal, and it was only the violent wobbling of his human support that warned him that Noel would not endure his weight many more seconds.

"Hold tight," he whispered, as he knelt and slipped a leg either side of his friend's neck.

Noel managed to stagger a few feet away from the nettles, then he stumbled and fell, crashing Malcolm upon the ground. Both rose rubbing aching elbows.

"My feet are crushed," complained Noel, struggling to wrench off the boots. "Why must Gwen wear such small boots!"

"Because her feet are small," grinned Malcolm.

"Anyway, see anything?" demanded Noel, smiling again now that he bathed his naked feet in the sun.

"Tell you later," whispered Malcolm. "Let us away to our comrades for I have much to tell."

"I say, don't be a rotter," protested Noel. "Tell me."

"I've seen what none of us would have suspected," admitted Malcolm, solemnly. "Don't rush for our comrades, for we are being watched. The cliff is alive with Preventive men."

Malcolm Brewster acted as though they were really in peril.

"You go first while I keep an eye on the wall and windows," he ordered, a moment later.

"Right-ho, but do you really think we are being watched ? I say, it's all frightfully exciting . . ."

"If I had been seen, I would have had a bullet through my skull, but I was too cunning for them," breathed Malcolm, who had a vivid imagination and played games as though facing actual life. "Give the call of the gull when you're safe with our comrades and, whatever happens, wait until I join you all. You have food and drink enough to withstand a longish siege."

He stood sword in hand and, as it were, covered Noel's retreat as only a valiant comrade could, not relaxing until his brother smuggler gave his imitation of a gull cry.

It sounded remarkably like a choking cat !

"'Tis well I know the secret bridle path 'long which the laden pack mules breast the Downs," growled Malcolm to himself, fixing his sword in his belt and setting out upon his adventurous and lonely journey. "My trusty men will lament their chief if some traitor has placed an ambush for his undoing."

A hovering gull watched the boy creeping amid the bushes with solemn, bright eyes, for a moment, then swooped screaming over the sea.

Malcolm found his followers in a state of breathless

excitement. " 'Tis well I spied," were his first words, as they gathered round him.

" Chuck the story stuff and let us hear what you saw," demanded Noel, impatiently.

" Oh, let Malcolm tell his story in his own way," protested Gwen, enjoying the spirit of the game. Malcolm seemed to make everything so exciting. " It's lovely to feel it's real when it isn't. Isn't it, Dudley ? "

Thus appealed to, the youngest smuggler grinned, undoubtedly living a life so perilous that he was partly nervous and partly excited as he sat close to his sister. Now and again, he twisted the ends of his smudged moustache.

" Oh, it's ever so exciting," exclaimed Gwen, not in the least afraid though keenly living the part of a desperate smuggler lass. " But do be careful, Malcolm. If anything should happen to you . . ."

" Have no fear for me, lass," gallantly returned the bold leader, much liking her glance of admiration.

" Do tell us what you saw, and stop this rot ! " demanded Noel.

Quite a fierce argument began between the two elder boys, but Gwen very quickly calmed their ruffled feelings, and said it was " such great fun pretending ".

" Sorry, Noel," apologised Malcolm.

" All my fault, but I'm sure you saw something terribly exciting over the wall. It's written all over your face."

" I did ! To begin with, but for a lawn behind the

house and a path, the garden is like a jungle," explained Malcolm, gravely, his voice scarcely above a whisper. "To reach certain parts of the garden, you would have to cut through brambles and rose bushes . . ."

"Like the prince had to do to reach the Sleeping Beauty?"

"Yes, Dud, but don't interrupt," from Gwen, not even thinking it funny that her small brother's face was smudged with burnt cork.

"Yes, like the prince had to cut his way through," agreed Malcolm. "But that's not the most exciting thing I spotted either. On the lawn was a beautiful silk tent of gorgeous colouring, and in front of it was a man dressed like a kind of soldier. He walked up and down as though on sentry guard."

"What was he dressed like?" asked Noel.

"I can't exactly explain, but not like our soldiers, anyway. But neither is that the most exciting thing I saw," declared Malcolm. "From the gorgeous tent came a boy. I should say he is about my own age. He looked very fair, upright, and terrifically handsome. There was something very noble in the way he carried himself. The soldier presented arms as if he were royalty. The boy saluted, and then laughed. That was all. But somehow I am sure he is of royal blood."

There was silence for a moment or so.

"Perhaps he is a king!" exclaimed Dudley, deeply impressed.

" Don't be a little idiot," from Noel, hoping the very same thing himself. " Anyway, there is no flag flying above the house. And how could a king be here without anyone knowing it ? "

" He might at least be a prince, Mr. Clever." Gwen generally stood up for her little brother when Noel was superior towards him. " Let's pretend he's a prince. Oh, it's such fun ! " and she clapped her hands together.

" So he may be a prince," argued Malcolm, to Noel's astonishment. "Somehow, he looked very princely, for he was dressed in a soldier's uniform. Not one of those toy things. And even carried a real sword."

" I dare say," admitted Noel, in one of his practical moods. " But my kid brother has a soldier's uniform and fancied himself no end in it. That doesn't make him a soldier even."

" Anyway, Noel, you know when that foreign prince came to school last term, we all said he looked like one, though he was dressed in flannels like us."

Even Noel was impressed by Malcolm's argument. After some more talk, all agreed that perhaps there was a real boy-prince within that high, foreboding wall, a prisoner in the House of Golden Windows.

But for the time being, they could do nothing about it.

The hot sun made them feel drowsy, and disinclined to be active.

Malcolm mentioned lunch, and Mrs. Spraggart's contraband was spread on the grass.

After their meal, Malcolm suggested (he did most of the suggesting, being leader), that they should take the " Smugglers' Oath ", and sign their names to a promise he had written out. He explained that that meant, should any turn traitor, his or her life would be in danger, and that life would be ended if he or she met their betrayed comrades.

It sounded very serious and real.

Their swords were placed on the ground, their colourful handkerchiefs removed. Even Gwen's curtain rings in her ears had to be taken off.

It was clear to all that the oath would have to be made to Malcolm. But none could say whether Malcolm could swear himself in as a smuggler.

Little Dudley argued that as Malcolm could not be a smuggler until he had taken the oath, he had no right to wear the skull and cross-bones on his chest.

Gwen agreed with her younger brother, a little proud that he should be so bold.

Noel, feeling he should stand up for his brother and sister, told Malcolm to remove the skull and cross-bones. With his handkerchief, he wiped off the ship in full sail, with the result that his chest looked as though he had not washed it for weeks. That's the worst of burnt cork !

The right way of swearing-in the smuggler leader was talked over, and it was decided he should swear himself in.

Malcolm drew apart for the solemn rite, and they

heard him muttering to himself in a voice as deep as his fourteen years could manage.

Then Gwen, after he had signed the oath, crowned him with his bright handkerchief, and Dudley, on his knees, presented their leader with his sword.

Noel, feeling he should play some part in the rite, re-drew the skull and cross-bones on his friend's chest, which happened to be a very fine one for a boy of his years.

After their own swearing-in, they were to receive their " smuggler's name " from Malcolm, for it was felt no self-respecting smuggler would have himself called " Dudley ", or " Noel " or " Gwen " or " Malcolm".

Smugglish names, was Dudley's term.

What they did not realise was that all this grave business had been seen, closely watched in every detail, and much envied.

From an upper window of the House of Golden Windows, the lonely and princely boy, seen by Malcolm Brewster, watched them with longing, lonely eyes.

He was as tall as Malcolm but slimmer, and very fair, with blue, brave eyes.

Malcolm was right, there was something " kingly " about that boy, and however sad and troubled and per-plexed his young life was, as he watched, the sadness of his features passed away and he smiled, a boy again longing to play with those others on the cliffs beneath the summer sky, where the gulls called and glided.

That princely boy was very lonely.

He watched Malcolm being given his sword by the kneeling Dudley, and such a pretty, solemn girl knotted a coloured handkerchief around the head of black curls.

And to be with and of them, meant more to that watching boy than the crown that might one day be his, a crown that had made his life lonely and sad.

CHAPTER III

TWO LEADERS

As soon as Malcolm was declared leader of the smugglers, amid loud hoorahs, he swelled out his chest. For some moments, he looked quite fierce and commanding.

Gwen, in the depth of her loyal heart, wished Noel had been leader, but she admired the grandeur and strength of character which their guest showed by attitude and expression.

His voice, too, was strong and quite deep, at times almost as deep as a smuggler chief's voice should be.

Noel Strathmore frankly, and with a rousing cheer, declared his friend as leader. Until Malcolm had come, he had always been leader, and perhaps there was now a little envy in his heart.

And Malcolm thought the same thought, and felt his guest had the right to lead. Thus, it came about, that after Noel had been sworn in, he was promptly made " Prime Minister ", and as a badge of office, Malcolm gave him a sheath-knife.

It was a generous gift.

None questioned, in their excitement, whether in their social order smugglers appointed a Prime Minister. The gesture was accepted as a mark of honour, and loudly hoorahed by Dudley and his sister.

" Come, my good and faithful Walnut Will, stand on my right hand," ordered Malcolm, as amazing at choosing a name for his friend as he had been in creating rank and distinction. " Walnut Will " did sound a bit smugglish, Dudley declared.

" Walnut Will ! " protested Noel, with some spirit. " That's a rotten name. Doesn't sound fierce enough for a smuggler."

" It's quite right," frowned Malcolm, with a trace of regal annoyance in his voice. " All true and worthy smugglers are walnut . . ."

" But I'm not . . . exactly, anyrate ! "

" You'll be as brown as a berry in a few days," answered Malcolm. " Only men who rough it in the open, brave storms, and live hard lives are tanned walnut hue."

" I think it's a grand name," voiced Gwen, feeling

that after such a generous gift as a sheath-knive, Malcolm had earned her support. "And when you're brown, Noel, you'll look almost as handsome and strong as smugglers do in picture books. I think it's a grand name. . . ."

"All very well for you to talk, Gwen. You won't get a name like that!"

"Mutiny, to begin with," hissed their leader, clutching his sword hilt. "Avaunt . . .! Or should it be ' avast '?"

"Don't spoil the fun, Noel," pleaded Dudley, eager to hear what he was to be called.

"Oh, all right then, just to please you kids," answered Noel, cheerfully. "I could think of much better ones, though."

Gwen was the next member to be invested. Her voice trembled slightly as she made the oath and signed her name, "Lively Lass".

"Lively Lass"! She was pleased with it, though Noel said it sounded like a pet name for a horse.

Dudley, who was often afraid to speak up on his own behalf, never failed to do so when it came to the interest of his sister. He thought she should be called " Smuggler Queen ".

"Oh, but ' Lively Lass ' is much nicer," declared Gwen, the little peace-maker. "Heaps of smuggler women must have been called ' Queens ', Dud! I'm as bold and as daring as any of you big, strong men. If I see a Preventive man, let him beware!"

At which, Gwen waved her sword, and seemed so earnest that Dudley scarcely knew whether to be more proud of Gwen, who was gentle and yet so full of spirits, or of Lively Lass who clearly wanted to meet Preventive men and use her sword upon them.

"Jolly fine! You'd make a ripping smuggler, Lively Lass," declared Walnut Will, in happy spirits again. "And now get the kid done, then we can play."

"That's you all over, Noel, to be practical at the wrong moment," protested Lively Lass.

It was not often when Dudley looked defiant and refused his sister's support. Now, his eyes shone quite dangerously as he took the oath. He had always agreed to play games in which Gwen joined, but now he felt that as a smuggler he could not rightly expect his sister to look after him.

But his smugglish name displeased him : "Kunning Kid? I don't like that in the least. I'm not cunning and I hate cunning!" he protested, to the surprise of all.

"It's not a very nice name, is it?" hinted Lively Lass, torn between loyalty for her leader and sympathy for her young brother.

"Anyway, 'cunning' isn't spelt with a 'K'," Dudley told Malcolm, and then seeing a frown upon the leader's brow, added in a quieter voice : "If I may humbly and respectfully suggest to you, Leader."

"It's not for you to suggest anything, to begin with," sternly from the leader. "It's a good name, the kind of name a real smuggler would like to deserve. It doesn't mean you're deceitful or tell fibs, you little ass! It means you use your brain rather than muscle, which you haven't got much of. Cunning means ' skilful ', and it might have been spelt with a ' K ' in the old days."

" Oh, it suits you, Dud," Gwen declared, making peace again, not a little surprised her small brother had been so bold as to fight on his own behalf. " Cunning really means the knowledge and ability used in doing things. Only it's spelt . . ."

" Avaunt ! " shouted the smuggler leader, sternly. " I know how to spell. ' Kunning Kid ' looks more . . . more . . . Well, it's more smugglish than ' Cunning Kid '. Anyway, smugglers couldn't spell ! "

" Rather ! " agreed Walnut Will. " You're our leader, anyway, and what you say goes. But, what's your . . . your smugglish name ? "

" Fierce Fred," and their leader looked the part. " Come, come, the moon is not yet on the rise. We have a four-masted schooner to unload before the dawn. She stands in the bay. Walnut Will, you will scout for Preventive men from Sandy Cove to Windy Headland. Give three flashes of your lantern . . ."

" 'Ware spy ! " suddenly hissed Lively Lass, withdrawing her sword and pointing it towards the House of Golden Windows.

Not a moment too soon, for the stranger was almost upon them.

Doubtless, he had been listening. He faced coolly as

B

fierce a band of smugglers as were ever likely to be found on a warm summer afternoon. He held his head high, and stood proudly before Fierce Fred's scowl and Walnut Will's threatening stance.

It was the princely-looking boy whom Fierce Fred had seen over the wall. He was not wearing his soldier's uniform. In its place he had donned a bright shirt and a brighter handkerchief adorned his head, while his flannels were rolled up above his knees.

With ink, he had drawn the skull and cross-bones on his forehead.

"Pleese," he said with a foreign accent, "I haf come to play."

"Oh, what queer English you speak," remarked Lively Lass, not intending to be rude.

"I speek littel Englese," he retorted, a flush of annoyance spreading over his cheeks.

"Half a mo'," protested Fierce Fred, angered by the proud air of authority with which the stranger regarded them. "To begin with, you've no right to wear the skull and crossbones. That's cheek! Only the leader may, and I'm leader. Walnut Will! Lively Lass!! Arrest the spy!!!" Walnut Will stepped forward briskly, and Lively Lass rather unwillingly followed. The former clasped a hand upon the stranger's shoulder, which was rudely shaken off.

"Pleese, you I will not have with hand on my shoulder!"

But Fierce Fred was not allowing his command to be defied.

"Bind him. We will try him, my worthy comrades," he declared.

Malcolm set the example by clasping the stranger's wrists. No resistance was offered. Very proud and noble was the prisoner's mien.

The smugglers marched him behind some bushes, where it was intended to try and sentence him.

"Pleese, I wish for you to play with me," protested the prisoner, as though he were granting them a privilege.

"You pipe down and answer when you're spoken to," ordered Walnut Will, guarding the prisoner.

Lively Lass and Kunning Kid stood on either side of their leader, to protect him should the prisoner become violent.

"Name?" demanded Fierce Fred, in his most blood-curdling voice.

"You must not for to speek with me like that!" The prisoner's eyes flashed defiantly, and the bold tilt of his head made all the smugglers feel that in their presence was a born leader. "I will play with you; but you must not questions ask for me to answer. From a window I watched."

"Spying, eh!" grunted Fierce Fred, scowling. "You have condemned yourself, sirrah! Do you or do you not know what smugglers do to spies?"

"You must let me play," the stranger ordered. "I

am lonely and I watch before I come to you."

"I think we ought to let him," pleaded Lively Lass, afraid she would be thought weak, but her gentle nature came out on top. Smugglers, she knew should have no hearts but her own was beating fast.

"Stow it," sharply from Walnut Will. "He may be a Preventive man in disguise."

"I tell you, I play you with me," angrily from the prisoner. "If I am seen to be outside of the wall there will be trub-bel! You must let me go now in one moment or two. I will first issue orders for when we shall again meet."

"So you think you're coming here to boss us," hissed Fierce Fred, then in a more gracious voice—for, despite the prisoner's boldness, they liked him and there was quite a friendly feeling growing between them all—he added: "Your name?"

"I will tell you. And then you tell me about you all. You must be my friends. Ja! I ask you for to be my friends and you must not say 'no'!"

"Oh, can't we," retorted Fierce Fred, much impressed, however.

"My orders are not disobeyed."

"We'll see about that later. Let's have your story," demanded Fierce Fred, quite aware that his comrades were well disposed towards the prisoner, and that his own leadership would soon be in danger if this stranger joined the band.

The prisoner said that his name was Bertet Carlsen. He was very lonely, and wanted young friends to play with. But " trub-bel " would follow if it became known he had left the jungle-garden within the high wall. More he would not say.

" So you're really a prisoner ? " asked Walnut Will, in a friendly voice.

" I command. I am not told," proudly from Bertet Carlsen. " You no und'stand ! "

" You can't expect us to und'stand unless you tell us things," Fierce Fred pointed out, quite reasonably. " You were caught spying, and must clear your name before you can be a smuggler. You ought to know that if you know anything at all about smugglers."

" But smuggler bad man. He cheat the king."

Fierce Fred became very angry, and Walnut Will waved his sword quite threateningly above the prisoner's head.

" Oh, don't hurt Bertet," pleaded Lively Lass. " He is so lonely and I am sure he only wants to become one of us."

" Good for you, Gwen," spoke up Kunning Kid, admiring the stranger for his boldness. Indeed, his spirit was somewhat arrogant, but his manner seemed so natural, and to command his right, that none took real offence.

Fierce Fred, in his heart, was a little afraid that were the prisoner to become a smuggler, his own authority would very soon suffer, for it was plain enough that his followers were well disposed to add to their numbers, and impressed by the spirit of the stranger.

But, Malcolm thought to himself, by agreeing to accept Bertet, they might solve the mystery of the House with Golden Windows.

The very same thought was in Walnut Will's mind, and an exchange of glances between the pair resulted in a swift and mutual understanding.

" Release the prisoner," ordered Fierce Fred, in his grandest manner. " Well, Bertet Carlsen, as a member of the Devon Smugglers, you will now take the oath and become one of us ! "

Bertet found himself among friends and, though none realised it then, from that moment true adventure and danger began for them all.

Much of his arrogance and pride melted. He shook hands with them all, but refused to kneel before Fierce Fred when told to do so. Such a display was only over-looked and forgiven because Lively Lass appealed for what she called " clemency ", as Bertet was a foreigner and wouldn't understand the ways of Devon smugglers.

" You'll be known as ' Spanish Main ', and with that name you will sign the oath," ordered the leader. " If you can't spell it, I'll tell you."

The piece of paper was produced, and the burnt cork. The oath was taken, and the paper signed.

Lively Lass presented the newcomer with her sword,

proudly declaring that she would obtain another from the first Preventive man she met that very night !

Spanish Main said he must hide the sword, for if it were found on his person there would be " trub-bel ".

Mrs. Spraggart's contraband—what was left of it after lunch, that is to say—was produced, and they shared the feast. Great and grand plans were discussed, and it very soon became clear that Spanish Main made most of the suggestions and expected them to be followed, which they surprisingly did, even Fierce Fred.

" I come not ev'rytime," regretted Spanish Main. " You must not ask. You must not come to me. That will make trub-bel."

" Oh, keep your rotten secret to yourself," Fierce Fred answered, feeling a little " fed up " that he had allowed Spanish Main to make most of the suggestions for their next morning, and he had so willingly agreed. " But can't we one day run a contraband through your country ? "

" Oh, do lets," gleefully from Lively Lass.

Even Kunning Kid voiced a mild surprise, and showed real disappointment, when Spanish Main would not agree to such an exciting idea.

One way and another, time fled by.

When, at last, a smuggling campaign was agreed to, Spanish Main declared he must not stay a moment longer, or there would be " trub-bel " as it was his tea time.

So, hiding his sword amid the bushes, they watched him carefully approach the wooden door in the wall, after a promise that he would meet them again when they next came to the east cliff.

Somehow, with the departure of Spanish Main, all the fire went from their spirit of adventure. They did not wish to play at smugglers again that day.

They sprawled in the sun, and idly watched the gulls overhead, each thinking his or her own thoughts, but not saying a word.

Gwen and Dudley felt very sorry for the lonely boy. They were not in the least curious to know why there should be " trub-bel " if it became known he had joined the " Devon Smugglers ", and would not be allowed to invite them into the wilderness of a garden beyond the wall.

Malcolm Brewster felt rather peeved (which he kept to himself), that the stranger's influence had more than equalled his own.

He foresaw that were they to meet often, there would be a quarrel before long ; not that he did not like Bertet Carlsen, but because both would certainly want to lead.

Later, Malcolm was surprised to find that while he had thought about Bertet and of his own leadership being in danger, he had fallen asleep.

He suddenly awoke to find the others were still asleep.

Everything was very still, even the gulls. He did not wish to be a smuggler chief any more that day.

Anyway, it was time for them to return home, so he awoke Walnut Will, Lively Lass, and Kunning Kid.

CHAPTER IV

SPANYARD'S STORY

KUNNING KID, on waking up after his doze, declared he felt hungry. Lively Lass searched what remained of Mrs. Spraggart's contraband, finding an odd apple, three buns, a cheese sandwich, and several small cakes in a rather crumbly condition.

Smuggling was over for the day.

" Bertet Carlsen's a kid," said Fierce Fred, setting his teeth into an apple. He was not quite sure whether he was sorry or not that Bertet had joined them. " He's too much side for my liking. After all, he had a lot to say for a new chap. He spoke as if he had the right to boss us."

"I rather like him," admitted Walnut Will.

"He is awfully nice," frankly from Lively Lass. "And he's no more a kid than you are, Malcolm. It must be dreadful to be so lonely. There is something so grand and nice about him. When we get to know him better, he may not want to talk so much and, anyway, it seemed so natural for him to . . . well, to say the things he said, although, of course, Malcolm is our leader."

"Glad to hear that," muttered Malcolm, rather grumpily.

"Anyway, I like him very much and I don't think it's fair to talk behind one's back ! "

Dudley looked quite angry.

"Well, who's running Bertet down ? " asked Noel, stretched out on his back, eyeing the gulls and the blue sky. "It's only right we should let him join in our games. And, anyrate, we might get into the garden."

"He looks so sad and proud that I'm sure he has a wonderful secret," said Lively Lass, ignoring the comment about the garden, into which she was just as keen to go as any of them. "But it will be mean just to make a friend to get something out of him, if he doesn't want to talk about himself. I vote we don't try to find out anything. I'm sure he has a secret. He's lonely, and none of us would like to be lonely."

"Spoken like a good little girl," teased Malcolm, in a good humour again. "And I don't mind admitting, though he's got too much side by half, he's rather decent."

Gwen was pleased that Malcolm had nothing really nasty to say against Bertet Carlsen. She felt anxious, however, that two such headstrong, eager boys would not play together often without a quarrel resulting between them.

It was Noel who suggested a swim, and hinted that Gwen and Dudley had better go home. The suggestion was agreeable to all, for Dudley wanted to talk in secret with his sister about Bertet Carlsen, and Malcolm wished to sound his young host as to his opinion of the lonely boy.

"Don't mind, Gwen?" asked Noel, who was very fond of his sister. "If you'd rather we come along with you, we will, of course."

Gwen caught a wink from Dudley, and understood he wished to share some secret with her. It was her sweet nature never to assert her own wishes so, in high spirits, she set off home with Dudley.

The two elder boys watched them for some moments, then Malcolm proposed climbing down the cliff, and going along the shore. The idea rather took the breath away from Noel for a moment, but careful search led to the discovery of an easy descent, where the cliff had crumbled years ago.

It was quite easy, though rather exciting, to reach the beach down the landslide.

They undressed behind some boulders. From the beach, the cliff seemed to tower to a great height, and both felt not a little proud of their climb-down. At the foot, they paused to gaze upwards to what seemed to be a great height that reached up and touched the scudding clouds.

" Good effort that," rather boastfully from Malcolm.

" I would never have dared it without you ! "

" Oh, don't be an idiot," laughed Malcolm, and ran for the sea.

He was a good swimmer, so also was Noel. They had a race to the harbour and back.

" Now let's dry in the sun," proposed Noel, wading through the shallows, breathing deeply.

Stretched out, they found the sand almost unpleasantly hot to their backs. But it was nice to feel the sun's rays soak into their glistening bodies.

" I don't quite know whether I care for Bertet or not," suddenly remarked Malcolm.

" He's all right, though he was rather bossy, just like you are," laughed Noel, good humouredly. " Funny thing is, it seemed so natural for him to lead. I'm sure he didn't mean to give offence. After all, he's a foreigner."

" I'm British, and no foreigner is going to boss me," retorted Malcolm, proudly.

" Don't be so sensitive ! " laughed Noel.

Malcolm did not answer. He was jealous of Bertet, without realising it. Headstrong himself, he didn't like the same nature in others. His disposition was frank and lively, however.

" After all," he commented a moment later, " there is something rather princely about him. And I'm sorry for a chap cooped up in that jungle of a garden. I hope he will tell us his story."

" Rather ! " agreed Noel. " But it's hardly sporting of us to make a friend of him to get his secret."

" Perhaps not," admitted Malcolm, thoughtfully. " Anyway, we won't press him. Gwen and your kid brother like him all right. I say, let's stroll home."

" Plenty of time yet, Malcolm."

" Well, stroll along the beach," suggested Malcolm, feeling restless. " As we swum to the harbour, didn't you see Mr. Spanyard, with a fine model of a ship? He was on the harbour wall, quite close to where we turned."

" I didn't notice. I was too keen on whacking you," answered Noel. " I say, he might give us a row so let's go and ask. It will be some days before dad will buy us a boat. I wonder whether Mr. Spanyard has one going cheap ? "

They slipped on their shorts and, other garments slung across their shoulders, strolled beneath the white cliff, rugged and towering, seemingly touching the sky.

They jumped over the smaller boulders.

The sea was smooth, except for the white-crested ripples that flowed over the sands.

The few cottages they could see were startlingly white

in the glare of the westering sun. . The grey harbour-wall was crooked like a giant arm about to embrace the little cove, and above it the masts of the boats rose like lances of an unseen army.

Malcolm was in a gay mood again, perhaps a little sorry that he had felt resentment against Bertet Carlsen. His laughter was loud and pleasant, echoing off the cliff in peal after peal ; and Noel was no less happy.

They found Mr. Spanyard at the harbour wall, dressed in serge trousers that smelt faintly of fish and seaweed, and a snow-white singlet that revealed bronzed arms, knobbly with muscle.

He greeted them with a smile, and went on working at the upper main royal sail of the model windjammer he had made.

It seemed wonderful to the watching boys that his thick, strong fingers could do such delicate work, for the riggings were of thread, and the perfectly-shaped yards were no thicker than match sticks.

All her fittings were in correct detail ; the wheel and catted anchor, the galley smoke-stack, and winches for veering the yards, even to the minute figurehead beneath the bowsprit.

"You're both looking tanned already," he greeted them, standing back to consider the work he had done. "I've only the sails to bend, and a touch of paint here and there, then she's finished."

The two boys asked a hundred and one questions

about her riggings and fittings, while he answered as the three sat on the wall, their legs dangling high above the incoming tide.

The House of Golden Windows stood out sharply against the skyline, its windows grey. Soon, however, the lowering sun would gild them and give beauty and a fairyland touch to the sad, sombre mansion.

Now and again, one or other of the chums glanced towards *the house*, and saw the windows gradually change until each pane was a sheet of burnished gold.

" Strangers don't come here often ? " asked Malcolm, eventually.

Mr. Spanyard had become silent and pensive, his keen eyes fixed on the horizon, as though seeking secrets only to be found by brave voyagers and explorers.

" Not often, and they're not made welcome," the man answered. " This is a quiet, dull old place, where there is no haste, no anxieties. Goodness alone knows how they make a living, but they seem to be happy enough."

" You live here, Mr. Spanyard, so you ought to know," remarked Noel. The golden windows held his eyes. He added, in a quiet, curious voice, " That house looks like a fairy palace now."

Mr. Spanyard glanced towards the east cliff, and shook his head sadly. " There is something happening up there, but it is best not to try to find out about it. No one hereabouts knows what is happening up there, but they all know there is a story worth the telling."

"Oh, you might tell us," urged Malcolm, eagerly.

"I know nothing to tell," declared Mr. Spanyard, in a quiet voice. "There may be a story to tell, but no one knows it. The gates are kept closed and locked. Very seldom visitors come in swift cars, with blinds drawn down. The local folk are simple and ignorant, which is why they are superstitious and suspicious. They seldom even pass the place, and when they do they hurry by. It would not surprise me if they never pass that place at night."

"We played on the east cliff today, Mr. Spanyard. And I climbed on Noel's back to look over the wall."

Malcolm immediately regretted he had spoken. Too late, Noel had thrown him a warning glance.

"I shouldn't look over the wall again if I were you," warned Mr. Spanyard, rather sharply. "It may even be dangerous to look over the wall. They say strange things have happened up there of a night. A stranger was found unconscious, at the foot of the wall, one morning. That was not so very long ago. It was thought he might have been spying."

"I . . . I didn't see anything much," said Malcolm, embarrassed. "Only a garden that made me think of the brambles and growth that surrounded the Sleeping Beauty."

Mr. Spanyard did not seem to be interested in Malcolm's remark. He was thinking his own thoughts, which he revealed to them after a silence of some minutes.

"One night, not so very long ago, a ship without lights stood off this shore, and men landed from a rowing boat," he told them. "Its rowlocks were muffled and oars too, so that without a sound it came in to under the cliff.

"Men climbed to the top, so it was said, for old Peter Rungate and his son saw them as they came home very late from Frigate Cove.

"You see, their way was over the cliff, and they had stayed too long before setting out for home, for none like to pass *the house* during darkness.

"Old Rungate said they saw some men creeping towards the wall, so they hid behind some bushes. It was too dark to see much what happened. They thought they heard sounds of a fight, and the men who had landed from the boat ran away down the cliff. Next morning, a stranger was found unconscious on this side of the wall."

"But who saw the ship off-shore that was without lights?" asked the interested Noel. "You say it was too dark to see much, and old Peter Rungate and his son came over the cliffs. They wouldn't have seen the ship in that case."

"That's how the story runs, young man," answered Mr. Spanyard, not pleased by Noel's comment.

The shadows were lengthening, and the windows of flashing gold were gradually turning to pale yellow. Two men were preparing their boat for going out on the tide later, and a few idlers were lounging on the wall close to where the nets were spread to dry, on the edge of the cobbled road.

" *The house*," resumed Mr. Spanyard, a few moments later, " is not so old as it looks. It was built by a foreigner some years before 1914. A spy lived there, and it was said many ships were torpedoed off this coast because of his treachery.

" The man who then lived in *the house* was said to send information hereabouts to the enemy submarines off the coast. That is why the local folk hate the place. It's still evil, they say. Keep away from *the house*, and the local people will become quite friendly."

" Oh, well, we can't do any harm," voiced Malcolm. " Anyway, I don't suppose we will look over the wall again. There's, nothing interesting to see."

" Don't go near the place unless you want bad feeling to be stirred," warned Mr. Spanyard. " They said *the house* can do harm. It was empty for a long time after the great war and then, about a year ago, someone came there, but they are never seen. They don't shop here. They live in a world of their own. No one knows anything about them."

Mr. Spanyard slipped off the wall, to stand and gaze up the cobbled road. Everything was dusky and quiet, even the lapping of the tide that scarcely muttered amid the fishing boats.

" You lads are foreigners to these folk," he told them, in a quiet voice. " They won't welcome you. And if you do talk with them, don't ask questions about *the house*."

The House of Golden Windows now looked drab and mysterious against the twilight sky. Here and there a light gleamed from a cottage window, or a fire glowed through an open door farther along the cobbled road, away from the harbour.

It was so still that life itself seemed to be settling down to a long sleep. The few local youths and men gathered, by the spread nets, did not talk. The men solemnly smoked their pipes, and gravely stared into space.

"You are really a stranger here, Mr. Spanyard," remarked Noel. "You don't talk like they talk. Don't you find it lonely?"

"It won't be lonely any more if you lads come for a row now and again," he answered. "Or for a swim. And I can teach you to box, or to make a model ship. By the way, the father of one of you boys hired a small boat from me today. She's down there close to the steps. She's yours whenever you want her."

With which remark, Mr. Spanyard picked up his model, and strode towards his cottage.

Mention of the hired boat excited the boys. They descended the steps to examine her. She was a stout Peter boat (so Mr. Spanyard told them later), with two sets of oars.

She was drab, and smelt of fish and tar, but it was their craft and they were delighted by such a possession.

Stepping aboard, Malcolm eagerly examined the small

fore- and aft-decks before electing himself captain. Noel accepted the rank of lieutenant without protest.

They both agreed that when she was used as a smugglers' craft, their smugglish names would be used, but at the moment she was part of the King's Navy.

Captain Malcolm declared that she would carry sail to advantage, and Lieutenant Noel agreed, respectfully suggesting that the naval dockyard, at His Majesty's port of Syre, should fit her out without undue delay.

They decided to consult Mr. Spanyard the following morning.

As they strolled homeward, they bade " good-night " to the shadowy figures lounging by the nets, and received only stony stares in exchange for their politeness.

Women at the cottage doors glanced at them without interest.

Even the children, not yet abed, showed no interest in them.

Such a stern and foreboding conduct towards strangers gave a deeper meaning to Mr. Spanyard's words : " It won't be lonely any more if you boys come for a row . . ."

They realised the pleasure their friend had found in the long and tedious task of making a model of a windjammer.

" There is a mystery about Mr. Spanyard," suddenly remarked Malcolm, as they entered the drive leading to their house. " What keeps him here, and why did he ever come ? It's a cock-eyed place to be lonely in ! "

Noel did not attempt to find an answer.

Mrs. Spraggart called them " little savages " as they entered the house, wearing only shorts, their chests still bearing faint smudges of their recent tattooing with burnt cork.

She shooed them upstairs to the bathroom, as though they were wayward chicks late for the hen-house.

After supper, Mr. and Mrs. Strathmore played hide-and-seek in the gloomy garden with the children, and then Dudley was ordered to bed.

Gwen went also.

From her adjoining bedroom, she told him a story of a prince who lived in The House of Golden Windows.

CHAPTER V

'WARE TRAITOR !

FIERCE FRED and Walnut Will decided that to be " Devon Smugglers " without a boat was unthinkable.

Thus it came about next morning, before breakfast, the gang assembled in the old summer-house on the edge of the cliff-garden. And there they decided that the boat must be got ready for " sail and oar " (Noel used that expression as though it was a sailor's term only known to the most experienced of seamen).

She was to be painted a " brave red ", declared Malcolm, who was doing most of the talking and all the ordering.

Gwen, who loved the sea and was really excited about having a boat to themselves, was chosen to launch her as soon as she was ready for the Seven Seas.

Dudley said very little during the exciting chatter. Anyway, had he done so, possibly very little notice would have been taken.

Gwen took it for granted that her small brother would agree to any plan suggested, and she did not ask him for his opinion of the grand ideas until they were seated at breakfast.

"All right, I suppose, Gwen. But I can't stand the smell of fresh paint. It makes me feel sick."

When they were about to set out for the harbour after breakfast, Dudley could not be found anywhere. They went without him.

Mrs. Spraggart had packed lunch, and quite crossly she told them not to worry her until tea time, for she had quite enough to do without having "chicks cackling and fluttering" under her feet all day, that she had!

"But we can't find Dudley," exclaimed Gwen, being shooed from the house.

"Master Dudley has taken his books and lunch and gone off on his own."

Gwen felt a little disappointed, but she had known Dudley to behave equally strangely before. She supposed he was in one of his lonely moods.

Anyway, he couldn't stand the smell of new paint!

Fierce Fred, as a smuggler, considered that Kunning

Kid left much to be desired, a remark that began an argument with Gwen, which only ceased when the harbour was reached.

In her heart, Gwen thought it was a little mean of Dudley, for he might have told her.

Mr. Spanyard was consulted.

He suggested the boat should be hauled from the water and turned bottom up. He promised to supply red paint and brushes, and offered to help them to step a mast and make sails later.

Indeed, while the two boys painted her, Mr. Spanyard and Gwen became busy cutting old sail cloth, and stitching it together to make a gaff and jib.

By tea time, much work had been done.

Mr. Spanyard thought that the following day they could set the mast and rigging, and even make a trial run to Earlie Cove and back.

Her name, it was decided after much discussion, would be *Gallant*.

She was to be christened by Gwen, who would break a bottle of gassy lemonade over her bows. They had seen a news reel of the launching of a giant Atlantic liner, and knew all about how to send forth a gallant ship upon her mission into the Seven Seas.

On their return home for tea, Mrs. Spraggart regarded the paint-bespattered boys with horror, throwing her arms into the air and giving a little scream. Knowing that they had set off to paint the boat, she expected nothing less than red from head to heels, and Master Noel's " only pair of flannels " ruined.

Bronzed and red-speckled, the two boys looked quite dreadful beings.

She shooed them upstairs to the bathroom, as happy as they were, and set about getting tea ready.

When Dudley returned, he heard all about the *Gallant*.

He was ordered to be present at the launching at four o'clock precisely following the next afternoon.

For the grand launching, Malcolm had decided to call himself the " Lord Mayor of Liverpool ", and said he must deliver a speech of welcome when Gwen arrived to launch the ship.

Mr. and Mrs. Strathmore received invitations, and Mrs. Spraggart was asked to make a special cake, and promptly snapped:

" What time have I got for making cakes ? " she told them, and went to the kitchen to begin operations.

Later, she was asked to be present, and seemed very surprised by the honour paid to her, and delighted to accept.

" Me, a 'umble old body ! " she said, breathlessly, then added : " Bless my chicks, I haven't a dress fit for a launching."

Within an hour of tea being over, the plans for the launching had grown so important in the minds of the children that Malcolm drew Noel aside and whispered that, as Gwen was to launch the *Gallant*, someone must present her with a bouquet.

Malcolm had talked himself almost hoarse, and gave orders to everyone and anyone who would listen, so eager was he that the ceremony should come off without a hitch.

Indeed, it was to be a great event, which even Mr. Strathmore permitted to interrupt his work.

A picnic was decided upon, opposed by the good Mrs. Spraggart, but they all knew she would half empty the larder rather than fail her " chicks ".

The two elder boys saw Mr. Spanyard that evening (after Dudley had gone to bed and Gwen, as usual, was telling a story), who was invited and was asked to " receive " the guests.

On the morning of the great day, Malcolm, Noel and Gwen were away early.

Dudley was told to make a bouquet and present it to Gwen after the " Lord Mayor of Liverpool " had made his address of welcome to her at four o'clock precisely.

Mrs. Spraggart appeared at breakfast with her hair in curlers, which was always a sign of something important about to happen, and that she was minded to look her very best.

She thought the domestic staff and the gardener should be invited.

It was impossible to launch the *Gallant* down a slipway, so it was arranged to refloat her at the foot of the steps, and the christening was to be performed before casting-off.

Everything was ready for the launching long before the appointed hour. The two elder boys slipped on their bathing costumes and had a swim, after which they dressed as smugglers in the most gorgeous remnants Mrs. Spraggart had been able to sew together during the baking of the special cake.

Mr. Spanyard produced some real old cutlasses, and two big highwayman pistols, which he gave to the boys. He even displayed a Union Jack to mark the occasion.

The local inhabitants gathered some distance off, staring and saying nothing. Some of the braver children approached, eyes large and round.

The *Gallant* looked very grand in glistening red, with snow-white gaff and jib ready to be hoisted.

How Malcolm satisfied his imaginative mind that he could be the "Lord Mayor of Liverpool", while gorgeously arrayed as a "Devon Smuggler", only himself understood.

However, he wore a dog chain round his neck, that had been brightly polished by Mary the maid, and his sash bristled with small arms. Impatiently, he awaited the hour of four o'clock, rehearsing his speech.

The domestic staff and gardener from the house were the first to arrive, heavily laden with Mrs. Spraggart's tea. Then Mr. and Mrs. Strathmore appeared, with Mrs. Spraggart all in her very best and beginning to look important.

She was dressed, in her own opinion, fit for a royal launching. She carried a bouquet so large that one could well imagine that not a flower was left in the garden.

Dudley, however, was not there. He had gone off on his own early during the afternoon, and had not been seen since. His absence angered the lord mayor, just when everything seemed to be going according to plan.

Gwen waited in Mr. Spanyard's little cottage, peering from behind the partly closed door, and feeling quite sick with excitement. She was not to appear until all the guests had arrived.

The local folk crept a little nearer and formed a background of staring eyes and stolid faces, roughened and tanned by the elements, while the children transferred their attention from the smugglers to the tea that was being unpacked on the harbour wall.

Dudley, or no Dudley, the " Lord Mayor of Liverpool " was only waiting for four o'clock to be struck on the ship's bell by Mr. Spanyard, and then the launching would begin.

Mrs. Spraggart bowed so low on being received by the lord mayor that her dress burst a seam, and she was plainly heard to say : " Drat ! "

Mr. Strathmore removed his hat, and most solemnly presented Mrs. Strathmore. It was at that precise moment when the stranger arrived. He was the " foreign-looking " gentleman who had spoken to Noel and Malcolm on their first night down at the harbour.

" Count Aland," he introduced himself, and entered into the spirit of the game so thoroughly that Noel forgot he disliked the stranger.

Mr. Strathmore explained to the Count the nature of the ceremony, and that they were waiting for " the lady who was to launch the ship ".

" I'll punch Dudley's silly head," Malcolm whispered to Noel. " He's spoiling everything ! He is supposed to present the bouquet to Gwen."

" You leave him to me ! "

Dudley, however, did not appear, and it was Mrs. Spraggart who saved the situation when the great moment came to receive Gwen.

" It must be quite four o'clock," restlessly from Noel.

It seemed to be very much later than four o'clock when Mr. Spanyard struck eight bells, which aboard a ship would have marked the beginning of the dog-watch.

Gwen came rather bashfully from the cottage, a curtain making a train that picked up a lot of dust on its way to the launching. She wore a blue shirt and red shorts, with a rainbow sash in which were stuck one pistol, two cutlasses, and a dagger of wood.

Red cloth overlapped her wellington tops, and Noel had made a wreath of daisies for her hair.

Her cheeks were almost as red as her shorts.

One or two of the children raised a timid " Hoorah "

The " Lord Mayor of Liverpool " stepped forward and delivered an address of welcome, saying by mistake : " . . . that such a face could launch a thousand ships ! " which caused laughter.

Then he presented the " key of the city ", borrowed

from the bathroom on a strict promise it would be returned that evening.

Gwen was almost in the act of launching the ship, when Dudley's absence brought Mrs. Spraggart into the limelight, to her evident joy.

She was to present the bouquet. Approaching Gwen, an extra low curtsy caused another seam of her dress to go, and once again she was plainly heard to say : " Drat ! "

Then, escorted by the " Lord Mayor of Liverpool " and Captain of H.M. Speed Boats (who was Noel, for none was actually a smuggler until the ship was launched), the trio approached and descended the stone harbour stairway.

At the foot of the stairs and close to the boat, stood the Master Shipwright of Liverpool (Mr. Spanyard in white canvas trousers and blue-and-white ringed jersey). He was presented.

At this point, Mr. Strathmore made a little speech on behalf of the directors of the company that had built the *Gallant*, handing her over to the " Devon Smugglers ".

The bottle of gassy lemonade (first shaken by the " Lord Mayor of Liverpool " to make sure it would go off with a loud bang !), exploded like a penny fire-cracker, and Gwen shouted : " I name thee *Gallant*. Good luck to you wheresoever you are upon the Seven Seas ."

Count Aland, thereupon, raised his peaked yachting cap and cheered, and the local children (who had crept nearer to where the tea was spread along the harbour wall, on a white table-cloth), cheered also, and several of the old men raised their caps and hats because the count had done so.

Then, as planned, the " Lord Mayor of Liverpool " vanished and in his place stood Fierce Fred, waving a sword as he leapt aboard to unfurl the skull and cross-bones at the masthead.

Walnut Will exploded a pistol which Mr. Spanyard had kindly loaded without shot, and Lively Lass, tossing off her curtain train and crown of daisies, jumped into the boat, and scanned the harbour waters with her right hand shading her eyes, looking no less fierce than the other rascals.

" Cast off, my hearties ! " yelled Fierce Fred.

The breeze, such as there was, was fortunately favour-able, and they sailed once round the harbour, for Earlie Cove was too distant for a trip before tea, and landed amid cheers and waving of handkerchiefs and caps.

The absence of Kunning Kid was not remarked upon. Even Lively Lass felt angry with her brother one moment, and anxious the next.

Mrs. Spraggart appeared to be quite afraid of the smugglers. She bribed them with cakes and lemonade, keeping fearing eyes on their weapons, and breathlessly saying that she was only a poor old woman with nothing worth taking on her.

Tea was provided in such abundance that the staring children were invited to share it.

Count Aland, his English peculiar and somewhat broken, became very friendly towards Noel and Malcolm. Indeed, he put himself out to be pleasant. But the two boys liked him even less than on the night when they first met.

"My young friends," he remarked, taking his fifth sausage roll, which Noel considered was bad manners. "It dis of great plee-sure I you guest can be. We must be friends very firm. Pleese, could I a smuggler be with you?"

"Well, no, you can't very well," promptly answered Fierce Fred, who had a toothbrush moustache from a piece of rabbit skin, and was busy twirling the ends.

"Oh, no, no, no, pleese do not say that," protested the count. "It dis mooch dis-appointment you fill me."

"His mooch dis-appointment" did not spoil his appetite, however, and later an indignant Mrs. Spraggart expressed her mind when they returned home : "I thought that for'n gentleman would never stop eating. My poor chicks were starved !"

Before tea was over, Count Aland mentioned in a whisper so that only the two boys heard—*the house* on the east cliff, its windows gradually turning pale yellow, and would soon be burnished gold.

He asked whether they had found out who lived there.

Neither Noel nor Malcolm answered.

Dudley fortunately appeared at that moment, to be coldly received by the "Devon Smugglers".

He looked a little crestfallen, and became more so as Lively Lass gave him what she called "a withering look".

The windows of *the house* were golden when Count Aland bade all farewell, bowing very low as he shook hands with Mrs. Strathmore.

Mrs. Spraggart plainly did not like him, and sniffed as he bowed coolly in her direction.

Dudley kept close to his mother as they walked home, anxious because the "Devon Smugglers" so plainly disapproved of his conduct.

If only Gwen had smiled in his direction, he would have felt happier.

"We didn't mind you not helping to paint the boat as the smell might have made you sick," Gwen told him as the party went up the drive. "But it was horrid of you to be away from the launching. You could have helped with the sails. There is no excuse, Dudley, so don't try to say anything." Gwen hastened ahead to join her brother and guest, leaving Dudley feeling very miserable and guilty. He felt that he had done a great wrong No more was said to him until after supper.

"Come to headquarters for trial," ordered Fierce Fred, in quite a blood-curdling voice.

"Headquarters" was the old summer-house on the cliff.

"And be smart about it," added Noel. "You've got to be in bed soon."

Dudley hesitated.

He did not mind so much that Noel and Malcolm were

c

angry with him, but that he should have hurt Gwen's feelings was quite another matter.

Dudley found them waiting for him in the old summer-house. It was gloomy there, and a lighted candle, stuck in the neck of a bottle, made the scene even less cheerful.

Instantly he appeared, Walnut Will and Lively Lass fell in on either side, cutlasses drawn and plainly not in the mood to tolerate any nonsense.

"Prisoner, you are suspected of having secret meetings with the Preventive men."

Dudley held his head high : " I am a true smuggler. As true as any of you ! "

"So you say and, anyway, it's bad form to brag," retorted Fierce Fred. "Where have you been and what have you been doing this afternoon ? "

Dudley licked dry lips, and hesitated to reply.

"You will be tortured unless you speak the truth," threatened Walnut Will.

Gwen pressed her lips and felt very sorry for her young brother, but she was determined he should be punished. She knew she dare not catch his eyes pleading for her help, so kept her own lowered.

"You have gone off alone at sundry times," gravely from Fierce Fred. "And in secret."

"Hurry up ! " ordered Walnut Will, impatiently. "You've got to clear off to bed shortly."

Dudley did not lack courage.

"I am a true smuggler," he answered. "I give my

solemn word of honour I have not spoken to any Preventive men."

" Then where have you been ? " demanded Fierce Fred, mercilessly.

" I have sworn never to reveal ! "

For some moments there was an uneasy silence. Walnut Will suggested they should hold a secret conference, and they went outside the summer-house.

A moment or so later, they returned, grim and much displeased with their prisoner's conduct.

" Devon Smugglers keep no secrets from each other, Kunning Kid," voiced Fierce Fred, scowling. " You must prove there is no stain upon your character. We will give you time in which to think."

" I have promised never to say," pleaded Kunning Kid, in a trembling voice. " You mustn't ask me to break a promise."

Curiosity rather than suspicion was keenly aroused.

Gwen, particularly, was hurt that Dudley should keep a secret from her. Out of the corner of her eyes, she saw that he held his head high, and was clearly determined to keep his secret.

She felt that she had never loved him so much as at that moment.

The youngster was torn between two loyalties.

" Oh, Gwen," he said, appealingly, " I am a true smuggler, and you wouldn't have me make a promise and then break it?"

" It's all very well to keep on saying that," sternly from Fierce Fred.

" But I did promise ! "

" Well then, who did you promise ?   We've the right to know that, Kunning Kid."

Dudley remained silent.   And through the silence came the voice of old Mrs. Spraggart calling her " chick ".

" Kunning Kid, tomorrow night, at the hour of sunset or thereabouts," ordered Fierce Fred, " you will appear for trial in the cave of the smugglers—by which I mean the attic—and unless you can then clear the suspected stain on your character, sentence will be passed."

Dudley flashed a defiant glance, the first of his life, and Gwen thought he looked very handsome and brave.

But she remembered in time that he had not behaved as a true " Devon Smuggler " should towards his comrades, and turned her head away from him.

Kunning Kid ran away in the direction of Mrs. Spraggart's voice.

He was almost crying, and Gwen dabbed a handkerchief to her eyes and gave a quiet sniff.

That night, Gwen did not tell Dudley a story, and neither did she go to bed when he did.

Dudley wept a little on his pillow after he had stared out of the window, determined to be loyal to a promise, though that would mean ceasing to be a " Devon Smuggler ".

CHAPTER VI

A QUEENLY LADY

DUDLEY was too sensitive not to feel hurt, distressed that he found himself torn between two loyalties.

He would not break his promise. Not even wild horses would drag from him what had happened to him during the afternoon of the launching.

He felt very, very miserable.

It was very quiet and shadowy in his bedroom. He could not even hear the tide lapping amid the boulders at the foot of the cliff just beyond the garden.

He crept from his bed, to curl up on a chair close to

the window.   Resting his arms upon the sill, he pressed
his chin upon them, and dreamily looked across the
tree-tops to the House of Golden Windows.

He felt very much alone as the shadows stole out upon
him from the corners of his bedroom.   A few birds sang
in the garden, that was scented by flowers.

The windows of *the house* flashed and flamed, sheets of
pure gold catching and throwing back the glory of the
setting sun.   The sky was cloudless, and the sea a serene
blue, so that it seemed impossible it could in its anger
rise and hurl great ships against the cliffs, as now and
again it had done.

On the following night he was to be tried, but he knew
he would keep the secret.

That meant even Gwen would not think him to be a
true " Devon Smuggler " any more.

It was the House of Golden Windows that was the
trouble.   It had come into their lives, and it was bringing
adventure and danger to all of them.

From the first moment when Dudley had been
fascinated by its flashing sheets of burnished gold, he had
come under the power and influence of *the house,* and its
history was to become a part of his life, and the lives of
the other children.

It was because of *the house* Dudley had not been at the
launching.   It was because of *the house* he would not
break a promise.

Dudley's secret was a very simple one, but to the little

dreamer, as he sat at his bedroom window—with the shadows creeping upon him—it was a very important secret, and to break one's word was very wicked.

For the life of him, he could not see why he should not keep his promise and remain a " Devon Smuggler ". It was almost as bad as being a grown-up !

He missed Gwen.

Dudley could not help thinking what a jolly thing it was to be a smuggler, and to sail aboard a ship like the *Gallant*. The desire to lead such a reckless and lawless life was wellnigh overpowering, not that he would ever make a bold smuggler, but he enjoyed himself as much as the others.

It was quite true that fresh paint did make him sick, and that he did like being alone with his dreams. But, the fact of the matter was that fresh paint and dreaming were excuses to go alone to where they had played smugglers on the east cliff.

He had not been disappointed. He had met someone he wanted to meet.

From the very first moment, when Dudley had set eyes on Bertet Carlsen, he wanted to be his friend, to be alone with him sometimes and talk about his dreams. He liked his brother very deeply, and also Malcolm, but he thought they wouldn't understand if he told them of his dreams.

Perhaps Gwen only listened because she was kind. Dudley felt that Bertet would believe in his dreams, as much as he did himself. He wanted to make a friend of Spanish Main more than anyone else he had ever desired. That was how he felt, and it was a feeling he could not help having.

When Noel, Malcolm and Gwen had so gleefully rushed down to the harbour to paint the boat, no less joyously had Dudley set out for the east cliff. He had lingered a long time by the door in the wall that surrounded that strange, sombre house.

Bertet Carlsen had come to him. He was dressed in a white shirt and flannel shorts, a fair, brave-looking boy, with blue eyes that were sad. There was something proud and defiant about Bertet that was natural, and not offensive and hurtful.

Dudley spoke of the boat. They crawled amid the bushes to the edge of the cliff, and watched the busy " Devon Smugglers " prepare their craft.

Bertet had not remained long that day, for fear of " trub-bel " if he were found outside the wall.

Just before leaving Dudley, he had commanded—his eyes flashed as he spoke—Dudley never to ask questions, or to attempt to enter the garden.

Dudley had remained on the cliff until tea time, hoping Bertet would come back. He thought of the exciting times they could have in the boat, and roaming over the cliffs. He had never felt quite so deeply about anyone else before.

Anything that Bertet would do, however daring and

dangerous, Dudley felt he would have the courage to follow.

In Bertet's company, his own personality and limitations ceased to be, and he seemed to become quite another person—like Bertet, but without his natural authority.

The next morning, that was the day of the launching, Bertet Carlsen had not appeared on the cliff until late in the afternoon. That was why Dudley was late for the naming of the *Gallant*.

Bertet proved to be eager to talk, but first made Dudley promise never to repeat a word or even to tell " the others " that they had met.

Though Dudley had simply said : " Honest Injun "— which was Noel's idea of a real promise—Bertet accepted the oath.

Then he talked of an oppressed people of a nation that might have been great and good. He did not name the nation, but spoke so feelingly of its people and customs that Dudley felt he must have lived there once.

Dudley asked no questions when the story was finished. But he felt he would like to go to the oppressed people, and destroy the evil tyrant who ruled it.

Bertet declared that one day, when he was a strong man, he would rescue that nation, and bring peace and riches to its people.

Very solemnly, Dudley confessed that he would like to go with his friend, whatever the risk, and Bertet had said that perhaps that would be possible.

Dudley wanted to ask about the tyrant, and how he

came to rule such people, simple and good, who only wanted to live in peace, and not make war and be cruel.

Suddenly, Bertet had exclaimed that it was late and there would be " trub-bel " unless he hurried away, again making Dudley promise not to tell anyone that they had even met that afternoon.

Now, in the gloaming, Dudley stared from his bedroom window towards the House of Golden Windows. He did so wish he had suggested to Bertet that, as they were all " Devon Smugglers ", they should share their secrets with Noel, Malcolm and Gwen.

Especially Gwen.

The windows of *the house* were paling, and no longer flashed quite blindingly. The stark whiteness of the cliff was changing to grey, and the garden below was no longer a blaze of colour.

Through the trees on the edge of the cliff, the sea looked green and cold.

It was very, very lonely up there, with troubled thoughts.

Dudley, at last, crept into bed.

He cried a little, for he could not break his promise to Spanish Main, and he felt that it was very mean to keep a secret from the others, especially Gwen. He would be alone all next day, and at night he would be tried in the attic—which Fierce |Fred called the " smugglers' cave ".

Before Gwen went to bed, she tip-toed into her small brother's bedroom. She wanted to comfort him and, at the same time, felt angry because a secret was not shared.

Fierce Fred had said, quite rightly, that it would spoil all the fun if they kept secrets from each other.

During breakfast the following morning, Noel and Malcolm talked about sailing to Earlie Cove and back. Old Mrs. Spraggart was asked to prepare " contraband ".

Gwen felt that it would be disloyal to the " Devon Smugglers " to sympathise with Dudley.

To their parents, nothing seemed amiss, and none was other than well disposed towards Dudley. He felt him-self to be very much a traitor, but put a bold face on his troubles. He even tried to be indifferent as Noel and Malcolm appeared dressed ready for their illegal trade, and sang " God Save the King " in defiance.

" Avast," growled Fierce Fred, " tonight in the smugglers' cave you'll sing another song, my fine lad ! And if you cannot prove you're not a traitor, then beware ! "

Dudley replied that he wouldn't play smugglers if they asked him. He set off for the east cliff shortly after breakfast, feeling not a little envious of the other three as they ran down to the boat.

From the cliff-top, and close to the door in the wall surrounding *the house*, Dudley could see the harbour mouth and the roof and upper windows of his home, with the garden rising steeply beyond.

With a feeling of loneliness and longing, he watched the *Gallant* sail, with Fierce Fred shading his eyes to scan the horizon as he stood boldly on the bow half-deck. He looked a very daring figure, stripped to the buff, a vivid green pair of old pyjama trousers rolled above the knees, and a bright sash bristling with small arms.

Lively Lass stood by the helm, her hair tossed by the light breeze, while Walnut Will—looking more tanned than when they had arrived—stood ready to be brisk when she went on the starb'd tack.

The *Gallant* scarcely moved and the light breeze, according to Fierce Fred—who should know—would not hold, my hearties.

To all intents and purposes, she looked an innocent enough craft, and only the three rascals aboard knew she was running a rich cargo to Earlie Cove, that would cheat the King's revenue of one thousand golden guineas clear.

The wind failed, however, sooner than expected and, from the cliff-top, Dudley saw the gaff sail sheeted home and oars were shipped. Now and again, through the hot stillness, their laughter reached him as he watched the placid sea feathered by their passing.

Suddenly, Dudley was aware that Bertet stood before him and had been standing by his side for some minutes— so he said—watching the smugglers' boat make for Earlie Cove.

" Pleese, you come here not alway alone ? " asked

Bertet. " Your friends will want you for to go sometime. I like your friends."

" They're not my friends," growled Dudley, as he enviously watched the boat. " They won't take my word of honour."

" Surely, that dis not so, ja ! "

" Oh, I don't care," mumbled Dudley, a little ashamed of a sudden fit of sulks and self-pity. " You are my friend, anyway."

" Surely," Bertet smiled broadly. " And friend also of Fierce Fred, Walnut Will, and your beautiful sister, Lively Lass. But I can only play when they come to the cliff-top. You und'stand, for I must be careful or there will be mooch trub-bel."

" Fact of the matter is, I'm Kunning Kid no longer. Tonight I am to be tried, in the smugglers' cave, as a traitor."

Bertet's eyes became grave and inquiring : " Pleese, I do not und'stand."

" Oh, it's a lot of nonsense really," answered Dudley, pretending he did not care in the least. " I promised I'd never tell anyone that I met you yesterday, and they say ' Devon Smugglers ' don't keep secrets from each other."

Bertet's anxiety, that their meeting should not be revealed, was plain to Dudley.

" You see," Bertet explained, " they may talk and be overheard. It must not be known I trust them. It is better say nothing or people may overhear ! "

" I can see that, but as they have met you, Bertet, **no harm** can be done by trusting them."

" Ach, but no ! You must not speak," impatiently from Bertet. " It dis better so, ja ! "

" I am going to keep my word with you, but tonight in the smuggler cave, I shall be named a traitor."

" Smugglers' cave, pleese, where dis that ? "

" You see that topmost window," explained Dudley, pointing to his home partly visible through the bent trees on the opposite cliff. " It's there, in the attic. There is a real cave along the shore, but we haven't used that yet."

" I do not want for you to speek, if you pleese."

" I promised you I would not, but it's rotten," answered Dudley. " I can't see that it matters, just between us all. Especially as we're going to play all kinds of games together, Bertet."

" I know, Ja ! But you und'stand they will ask of what was said to you, Ja ! Dis better say no-thing."

Kunning Kid did not appeal to the spirit of a " Devon Smuggler ", which Bertet possessed by virtue of his oath and name of Spanish Main.

" It dis ver' dif'cult," admitted Bertet, realising that Dudley would much rather have no secrets between friends. " What will they do for with a traitor, pleese ? "

" That depends if they're in an ugly mood. Traitors are shot and stabbed, or perhaps have an ear or something cut off. Smugglers, anyway, are cruel to a traitor. They have to be. Haven't you read about smugglers ? "

" A littel.   But, pleese, surely they would harm you
not ? "

Kunning Kid forced a hollow laugh, and shrugged his
shoulders.   He felt something of a hero at the prospect
of being martyred for a friend, and hoped Bertet was
impressed.

While talking, they had wandered to where the wall
turned towards the road, and both were startled to see a
car stop before the tall, rusting gates.   Bertet gave a
stifled cry, and pulled his friend behind some bushes, his
face white and troubled.

" Pleese, I must go for there trub-bel will be.   It dis
my dear mother."

Before Dudley could answer, Bertet Carlsen fled from
him and through the wooden door in the wall.

Taking a cautious peep round the edge of the bush,
Dudley saw one of the iron gates open, and a servant
approached the car.   A very beautiful lady alighted.   The
chauffeur removed his cap, and the servant bowed very
low.

Dudley caught a glimpse of the lady's face.   She was
gracious and queenly.   Her eyes were sad.   The gates
were closed immediately she had passed into the
garden.

" Pleese, you promise not to tell.   I should haf said not
she is my dear mother."

Bertet's alarmed face appeared amid the branches of a
tree on the farther side of the wall.   Dudley placed a

finger to his lips, and shook his head, not daring to breath a whisper.

"I command, not a word," ordered Bertet, and vanished.

Dudley returned to the edge of the cliff, from where he could watch the slow progress of the *Gallant*. But he felt little interest in the fate of the "Devon Smugglers" making for Earlie Cove, for the image of that queenly lady was vivid in his mind.

The House of Golden Windows became more mysterious. That high wall concealed a tragic fate, and somehow Dudley felt that Bertet Carlsen's story of a tyrant, who ruled a lovable people, was real, and that indeed his mission later in life was to free them.

In the shade of a bush, Dudley fell asleep, and for a time he forgot that that evening he was to be tried as a traitor.

CHAPTER VII

TRUE " DEVON SMUGGLERS "

" TWILIGHT " is the hour when a traitor-smuggler should be tried !

At least, that was Fierce Fred's opinion.

The real difficulty was whether old Mrs. Spraggart would allow Dudley to be out of bed at the last phase of twilight. She was generally stern about the roosting hour of her " chicks ". Luck, however, was with the smugglers, for Mrs. Spraggart's lanky, ginger-headed nephew, who was in an everlasting state of growing out of his clothes, unexpectedly appeared on his motor-cycle, and persuaded his aunt to ride pillion into Exeter. She was not expected to be back until quite ten o'clock.

It was easy to ask the favour of an extra hour from Mrs. Strathmore.

No sooner had the smugglers returned home, after a day's sailing, and learned of Mrs. Spraggart's journey, than Noel asked his mother to allow Dudley to stay up an hour later than usual.

There being no Mrs. Spraggart to say " Dear me, *no* ! ", and really mean it, and as both Mr. and Mrs. Strathmore wished to finish the sixth chapter of the new masterpiece that evening, they were left very much to please themselves.

After supper, they waited for the dusky hour of twilight, which they did in a state of subdued excitement and earnestness.

Mary, the maid, had seen to their tea and supper, and had told them to be good as she had a headache. They promised to have their baths and put themselves to bed, without being the least trouble.

Dudley did not think the extra hour was much of a " treat ". If he kept his secret to himself, they would consider him as being very mean, but to break his word of honour to Bertet Carlsen was unthinkable.

After tea, Fierce Fred, Walnut Will, and Lively Lass retired to the attic to make arrangements for the trial, before which the prisoner was escorted to and locked in his bedroom, where he was to await the hour of trial.

There was an old rocking-chair in the attic, that became Fierce Fred's judgment seat, and an old velvet curtain of faded purple, which he considered as being " impressive " as a cloak, and claimed that also.

Walnut Will elected himself as prosecutor for the " Devon Smugglers ", and Gwen was secretly delighted to hear she was to defend the prisoner. In order to do so, she was allowed to have five minutes' private conversation with the accused.

Noel said that prisoners always had a private talk with their " defence " before the trial.

Over and over again, Gwen thought over what she would say. She felt a little like crying, and thought it would be a very good idea to weep, for that might touch the heart of Fierce Fred. She would plead that one so brave and young as Kunning Kid should " not be plucked in the bud ".

Very frankly, she had missed Kunning Kid terribly during the run to Earlie Cove that day, where the contraband had been successfully landed. At the same time, her sense of unquestioning loyalty towards the smugglers would not allow her to support the behaviour of Kunning Kid.

There should be no secrets kept from each other.

Everything was ready for the trial, including a candle stuck in the neck of a bottle, and a child's broken playing-pen set up as the dock for the prisoner to stand in.

They had had supper, and their baths before they dressed as smugglers, " armed to the teeth ".

Now that it came to judging his brother, Walnut Will felt none too happy.

There was something so frail and so in need of being looked-after about Dudley, that made Noel feel rather miserable. He felt almost like he did when one of his pets died.

The twilight was touching the windows of *the house* on the east cliff, when Kunning Kid heard the key being thrust into the lock of his bedroom door.

He was dressed as a " Devon Smuggler ", except for a bright headband and weapons, both of which had been taken from him, even as an officer's sword is removed before his court-martial.

He was surprised to see Lively Lass alone. She tried to look very stern.

" Kunning Kid," she told him, with a noisy gulp, " I am your counsel for the defence. I have only five minutes in which to speak to you in private, and prepare my speech. Everything depends on what you tell me. I can only save you by knowing the truth."

Kunning Kid's lips trembled ever so slightly, and his voice certainly quivered as he bravely replied : " I would rather perish than break my word. All I can say is that I am innocent of being a traitor."

" That's a fat lot of good ! " muttered Gwen, miserably, looking upon the ground.

He was very proud and handsome at that moment, standing erect, with fists tightly clenched, head high and eyes flashing.

Gwen stole a glance. She thought he looked very noble and was proud of his courage. She remembered just in time that he was a "suspect", and she "Lively Lass", otherwise she would have flung her arms round his neck and openly cried.

"It must be proved that you are no traitor," she said. "That can only be proved by you telling me your secret, Kunning Kid. There is no hope otherwise and . . . and I don't want to be a 'Devon Smuggler' without you! So there!"

She dabbed her eyes with a handkerchief, and the next moment looked quite stern and angry.

"I'm not the least bit sorry for you," she muttered.

The prisoner fixed his eyes on the House of Golden Windows, visible through the trees at the edge of the garden, and felt proud of his martyrdom.

Lively Lass appealed to him to speak the truth with such earnestness, and a number of half-subdued sniffs, that his resolve wavered.

Fortunately for Dudley, Walnut Will appeared at the moment when Kunning Kid felt he could not resist his sister's appeal a moment later. He wanted to run into her arms and hug her, and she wanted to do the same to him.

Kunning Kid was escorted to the "smugglers' cave".

" I have done my best for you," warned Lively Lass, pouting miserably.

Walnut Will carried a pistol and sword. Clearly, he intended to have no nonsense from the prisoner for, in his gruffest voice, he ordered the accused to precede him from the room. That was after Dudley's wrists had been bound behind his back.

The " smugglers' cave " was shrouded in gloom, except for the stronger light by the window and the glimmer of the candle in the neck of a bottle set on an upturned box, that served as a table, behind which sat Fierce Fred.

Fierce Fred was robed in the faded velvet, and was " armed to the teeth ". On the table were the prisoner's sword and headband, and the written oaths each had signed on the cliff, in the shade of the bushes close to the high wall surrounding the House of Golden Windows.

The prisoner was helped into the playing pen, eyed fiercely by the judge, who stroked his smooth chin thoughtfully.

" Prisoner, at this solemn hour when your life perhaps hangs on a thread," warned Fierce Fred, in the coldest and harshest voice he could manage, " do you plead guilty or not guilty to the charge of betraying and turning informant against the lives, interests and well-being of the ' Devon Smugglers ' ? "

" Not guilty ! "

" Oh, splendid ! " whispered Gwen, for Kunning Kid had spoken defiantly. They were all surprised and suitably impressed by his conduct.

" The accused will be tried," ordered Fierce Fred, sternly.

Thereupon, clearing his throat, Walnut Will bowed low to the judge, and opened the case for the prosecution.

" Now, let it be known," he declared, with a dramatic wave of his hand, " that Kunning Kid did of his own free will and without influence or pressure make, declare and inscribe his mark to a most solemn and binding oath that henceforth he would be loyal, steadfast and true to the cause, business, and laws of the Most Active Order of Devon Smugglers . . ."

" Can that be proved ? " demanded Lively Lass, leaping to her feet.

" Indubitably," in a grand manner from Walnut Will, waving the signed oath above his head. " Furthermore, let it be known that the prisoner did, on the two days following taking of the oath, absent himself from the Most Active Order of Devon Smugglers without sanction, permission, or pleasure of the Most Active Order of Devon Smugglers.

" And when asked, commanded, and ordered to explain, state, and declare the nature, purpose, and motive of such two absences, the prisoner refused to answer, state, and explain the nature, purpose, and motive of his two absences."

Walnut Will paused, feeling rather impressed with himself. He pointed an accusing finger at the prisoner and shouted :

" Can you deny, contradict, and dispute the accusation made against you, sirrah ? "

Kunning Kid remained stubbornly silent.

"Silence is consent !" declared Walnut Will, addressing the judge. " Now let it be known that those comrades, loyalists and followers of the Most Active Order of Devon Smugglers share all secrets, otherwise they stand suspect, informers, and spies of His Most Gracious Majesty's Preventive Men who by their duty, active work, and intention are enemies to those of the Most Active Order of Devon Smugglers.

" There," Walnut Will raised his voice, very pleased with his performance, " unless the prisoner declares, states, and explains the nature, purpose, and motive of his two absences, he shall be sentenced."

Walnut Will bowed low, then made a cut with his sword at a moth that fluttered from Fierce Fred's robe and danced about the candle flame.

By this time, Lively Lass's eyes were brilliant with the light of battle, much more affected by Walnut Will's eloquence than was the prisoner.

She watched the judge, fearful that the speech had affected him against the interests of the prisoner. She had made up her mind to fight for her young brother, and felt a little angry that Kunning Kid looked so unrepentant.

" A traitor forsooth," voiced Fierce Fred, glumly.

" Avaunt," retaliated Lively Lass. "The accused must be heard, and his crime proved. He has not been heard, and neither has his crime been proved.

" Within the meaning of the law and complementary to the framework (she had heard that complicated phrase on the wireless, and was deeply impressed by it) of the Most Active Order of Devon Smugglers, no crime can be committed, perpetrated, or executed by absence unless such absence is proved as being traitorous, with the intent to injure or cause capture and disaster to a member or members of the Most Active Order of Devon Smugglers . . ."

" Good for you, Gwen," in an aside from Noel. " You are some orator ! "

" Silence in the court," shouted Fierce Fred. " Any more of this rowdyism and I will command the court to be cleared."

That sounded very much to the point, and Fierce Fred felt pleased with himself.

" On behalf of the prisoner, I plead not guilty." Lively Lass's voice was quivering with emotion. She was fearful that her effort would fail, and then the holidays would be spoilt, and all made wretched. " The prisoner has stated . . ."

" No, he hasn't. Not here, anyrate," denied Walnut Will, not quite liking the idea his sister would get the better of him, though he wanted his brother to be released.

For a moment, Lively Lass was embarrassed and then forgot her part : " You're beastly to say that, Noel, and spoil everything . . ."

" Order," shouted Fierce Fred, shocked by the lack of respect for his authority. " Who is this person Noel ? Unless that person can appear as a witness, what he might have said is not evidence."

Lively Lass admitted that no such person could be produced as a witness under the circumstances, and continued with less liveliness.

" As the court will hear," she said, " the prisoner is a true Devon Smuggler, and none more worthy. Kunning Kid did not absent himself from a running of cargo, but from preparing the stout ship *Gallant*, as fresh paint makes the prisoner feel sick. I will call upon the accused to speak for himself."

The prisoner had very little to say on his own behalf.

He confessed that he had had a secret meeting with a person not named, and that he had sworn never to reveal the identity of that person, or the nature of the information then given to him.

He declared eagerly that he was no traitor.

" Indeed, this is a distressing case. The most distressing case I have ever heard," announced Fierce Fred, whose duty it now was to declare the verdict and pass sentence, if he found the prisoner guilty. " I propose now to sum up."

He cleared his throat, and glowered at the prisoner, and noted that Lively Lass was compressing her lips.

"There is no qualified medical evidence to prove that fresh paint makes the prisoner feel sick, therefore, such a statement cannot be accepted as evidence.

"Anyway, the prisoner could have helped with the sails and riggings. The counsel for the defence, clever though her arguments have been, as clever as any I have ever heard in this court, has said nothing that could give rise to leniency.

"Within a few hours of making his promise in the presence of the brethren of the Most Active Order of Devon Smugglers, the prisoner became a renegade—which means one who deserts a party—and therefore, guilty of the charge. I will consider the verdict."

Fierce Fred rose, and proudly walked to the window, the court standing until he had retired.

He could see the dusky garden, the windows of *the house*, that gleamed pale yellow between the trees.

"Oh, Dudley, suppose you can't be a smuggler any more!" whispered the grief-stricken Gwen. "I cannot break my oath and leave them, but without you there won't be any fun."

"Can't you lot take my word of honour?"

"Can't you trust us, you little idiot?" demanded the irate Walnut Will. "You wouldn't like us to keep secrets from you. And it's going to be beastly without you, Dudley."

Kunning Kid dropped his head for the first time.

It was very still and solemn in the " smugglers' cave ", so shadowy now, except for the candle flame that danced and flickered as though as agitated as any of them in that room.

" When a chap gives his word of honour, Noel, he can't speak," protested the prisoner.

The minutes lagged.

" He's a long time considering the sentence," whispered Walnut Will, rather miserably.

Kunning Kid looked longingly at his sword and bright headband on the table, and thought of the exciting voyages he might have made in the *Gallant*.

" Walnut Will, come here," suddenly whispered Fierce Fred, who had been staring out of the window. Walnut Will joined his friend in an instant. " See anyone behind that laurel bush by the rose bed ? "

It was dusky in the garden, but Walnut Will saw a face peeping between the foliage of the shrub. It was Count Aland, of the goaty beard and shrewd eyes, that were as black as jet beads.

" Spying ! " gulped Walnut Will.

Both turned sharply as they heard the door hinges creak. Through the heavy shadows, they watched Bertet Carlsen enter. They stood speechless from surprise, and none dared to believe his or her own eyes.

Dudley was open-mouthed and speechless for a full minute.

" Queek, listen, if you pleese," the arrival whispered, as they clustered round him, Kunning Kid having climbed from the playing-pen with some difficulty, as his wrists were bound behind his back. " I come because I know my friend true is, ja ! I must be queek or there will be trub-bel ! I make Kunning Kid promise not for to speek. He meet me on cliff yes'day and this day."

Fierce Fred was the first to recover from sheer astonishment : " How did you get here ? " he demanded.

" Pleese, Kunning Kid he tell me you make him of a trial here. I must not stop. There will be trub-bel ! You let him be a smuggler, yes ! He is true."

" The prisoner is acquitted ! " announced Fierce Fred, and then seized Bertet Carlsen by an arm. " You wouldn't have risked coming here unless you were jolly sporting, Bertet. I can see you're dead scared of something."

" Surely, yes. I come through bushes ver' careful."

" There is someone watching," warned Fierce Fred, aware that their make-believe had become something very earnest.

The colour drained from the cheeks of Spanish Main.

" Walnut Will and I will show you a safe way home, so you won't be seen," promised Fierce Fred. " You'll be seen if you go down the drive. Is your life really in danger ? "

Spanish Main did not answer immediately.

" Pleese show me way," he said, gravely. " I would like

very much if you all me not see any more. I think it is better for you."

"You're in trouble and we're standing by you, Spanish Main," assured Walnut Will, stoutly. "Devon Smugglers don't let each other down. It's frightfully decent of you to come. Kunning Kid was in a bit of a fix."

Bertet smiled : "I must go, pleese."

Lively Lass and Kunning Kid were silent.

It was not altogether that dusky hour and the stillness that made them feel afraid. There was something happening which they could not understand. Something more than make-believe.

It would be a long time before they knew that the shadow of the House of Golden Windows was slowly creeping across their lives.

Even Fierce Fred, bold and reckless though he could be, was grave and not a little alarmed because Count Aland was spying on them.

"You must not come," warned Spanish Main. "There may be trub-bel. It dis dangeroose for me to leaf *the house.* We are friend again. Kunning Kid no more worry."

He turned, and hastened towards the door, Fierce Fred and Walnut Will following.

Dudley and Gwen stood motionless and silent amid the shadows.

CHAPTER VIII

A GIFT

BEFORE Spanish Main was allowed to leave the house, Fierce Fred searched the bushes behind which Count Aland had hidden. He was not there, but there were imprints of footsteps in the soil.

The three boys left the house by a side door, after Fierce Fred had reported that " the coast is clear ".

They hastened through the vegetable garden that ascended to a small wood of wind-blown trees.

Walnut Will said they could reach *the house*, on the east cliff, without passing through Syre. If they were very careful, there was little danger of being seen.

The late twilight was a great help, but open spaces

were not crossed until Fierce Fred had scouted ahead, and imitated an owl as a signal that it was safe for Bertet Carlsen to progress.

Once they had crossed the road from the village, there was less need to be cautious, for between them and *the house* the bushes were thick.

However, all felt relief when the wooden door in the wall was reached.

" Listen, Spanish Main," whispered Fierce Fred, " we don't want to know any of your secrets, unless you care to talk. We would like you to play with us whenever you like. It was frightfully decent of you to come and save Kunning Kid tonight. I think no end of you for that ! "

" Rather, it was frightfully sporting of you," agreed Walnut Will.

" Surely, ver' much I would like to play smugglers. Thank you."

" Good ! Tomorrow, we go to the smugglers' cave to plan a running . . ."

" Cigars, lace and brandy this time," interrupted Walnut Will, in a breathless whisper.

" Yes, surely, I und'stand. But how do I go to the cave of the smugglers, pleese ? "

" Take the slope down the cliff," explained Fierce Fred, " to the shore. Then turn right at the bottom, and walk along the beach for about two hundred yards. You will come to a huge boulder. Much bigger than any other. That hides the entrance to the cave. Lively

Lass found it by accident, when playing along the beach. We'll bring candles and lunch."

" If I can, I will come, ja ! It dis ver' dif'cult for me, but it dis hol'day for me and I am let for to be a-lone in the garden. Now, pleese go. You are all ver' kind."

Before either could say even "goodnight", Spanish-Main had closed the door upon himself.

" It's a bit exciting," admitted Fierce Fred.

Noel nodded.

They became two silent, grave, thoughtful boys, each stirred by a feeling that Bertet Carlsen was kept hidden in the House of Golden Windows, because it was dangerous to allow him any liberty.

In the eastern sky there were pearly streaks, and soon the moon would be riding high, silvering the sea and making the trees look very black and solid.

From beyond the edge of the cliff came the mutter of the tide at the full, lazily stirring amid the boulders.

" Let's go down and see that the *Gallant* is snug for the night," proposed Malcolm. " It won't matter being a bit late for bed just for once. I say, what do you think of Bertet ? "

" I don't know what to think, 'cept it was frightfully decent of him to save Kunning Kid."

They walked on in silence, along the crest of the cliff, threading their way in and out of the bushes. Here and there, between the gaps, they could see windows gleaming with the light of several cottages, and far out to sea

D

passed the starry points of some homeward-bound liner.

Syre itself seemed to be of another world. Not a voice. Not even the shadow of a human being on any of the windows bright with light.

The thatched old post office and general shop, the little inn snuggling amid the folds of the cliff, the few cottages, all resembled dusky outlines of a peopleless village, which soon would be stark and clear-cut in the moonlight.

There was not even Mr. Spanyard in the doorway of his cottage. There was no light there.

The fishing fleet was gone, and only a few small boats shivered almost unseeably upon the dark, opal waters, that now and again heaved a long, slow ripple that broke soundlessly into the parent body.

The *Gallant* was snug and made fast.

Sitting in the stern half-deck and whispering, the water smelt, to the two friends, cool and muddy. Possibly neither was conscious of their apparel, or that their colourful sashes were stuffed with small arms.

It was about Bertet Carlsen they talked.

Malcolm admitted that he was bossy, but that didn't matter. It was the first time Noel had known his chum to be bossed by a boy his own years without standing up for himself.

When the moon threw scales of silver across the sea— giving to the harbour waters the appearance of a huge mackerel—Malcolm proposed a swim, but Noel protested that it was too late. If old Mrs. Spraggart returned and found them out, it would make trouble for Mary.

Passing up the cobbled road, with here and there patches of moonlight that seemed comparatively glaring, they met Count Aland. He was leaning against the harbour wall, smoking a pipe, close to where the nets were usually spread.

" Ah, smugglers ! " he pretended to be very much afraid of them, but the two boys were irritated and not amused.

Both had a queer feeling that he had watched them go down to the *Gallant*, and had waited for their return.

" Good evening, sir," answered Noel.

" This delightful place draws me," declared the Count, pleasantly, but it was not that kind of pleasantness that pleased. " It is so isolated and peaceful. It seems impossible that once smugglers thrived here, and no Preventive men or honest citizen would dare come within a mile of the place."

" Wouldn't they, sir ? " said Noel, interested. " Was Syre a dreadful place once ? "

" Dear me, yes. Smugglers thrived here, and smugglers are desperate when interfered with. I came here to find out all I could about the place," explained the Count. " I want to write a book about Syre. The last cottage on the outskirt of the village is higher than the others. From its upper window, the harbour and sea and country for miles can be seen. It was once a smugglers' look-out. I am staying in that cottage for a few days."

" I am quite sure there must be secret passages and a peep-hole in a good many of the cottages. Smugglers were very artful and I am very curious."

He laughed, but Malcolm thought he was too curious to be pleasant. There was no excuse for having hidden in Mr. Strathmore's garden.

" I am finding out a great deal, for most of the people hereabouts have lived from father to son for generations here. I know how to get them to talk, for that is my business."

" They seem to be rather a queer lot to us, sir, and not in the least friendly," declared Noel, frankly.

" Oh, well, they've inherited secretiveness from the days when strangers were suspects, and Preventive men were their bitter enemies. Now, they have no secrets worth keeping." The Count paused, then added in a whisper that thrilled the boys : " Except one, and on that subject they will not talk."

Their curiosity was aroused.

" They will not say a word about *the house* on the east cliff."

" Perhaps they know nothing, or there may be nothing to know, sir," suggested Noel, not quite able to keep excitement from his voice.

" That's the queer thing, they know nothing about *the house*. That is why I am so curious," smiled the Count. " When there is nothing known about a house, there is always something interesting to find out, you know."

The Count was silent for a few moments, drawing at his pipe that glowed amid the shadows.

"You have made no friends?" he suddenly asked his young friends, in a suave, quiet voice.

"They're not easy to make," Noel answered, cautiously.

"Then it must have been my mistake. I thought I saw a boy enter your drive and make for the house. That must have been a good hour ago. Certainly, the light was not good and I may have been mistaken. I only caught a glimpse of him. He did not appear to be dressed like either of you, or like the local boys."

Malcolm elbowed his chum in the ribs, but Noel required no warning to keep a still tongue in his head.

"Did you call to see my father, sir? He's very busy writing a book and doesn't like to be interrupted." Noel thought that was a clever remark. A neat trap.

"I called to see the smugglers," jovially from the Count. "But, as you were entertaining, I thought I would not intrude. I waited for a while, interested in a bird's nest I had found."

"We asked no visitors this evening, sir," answered Noel, with a queer feeling the Count was not speaking the truth.

"Then I was mistaken," he answered, agreeably. "There are no other boys of your age holidaying here, and yet I saw—or thought I saw—a boy who most decidedly was not a local youth."

A moment's silence followed. The chums felt uneasy, and eager to get home.

" I really called to make a small gift which I thought would please you," the Count resumed. " You will want a souvenir of your holidays, and this will provide an interesting collection."

To Noel's delight and surprise, Count Aland gave him a camera.

" Oh, how spiffing, sir ! " he exclaimed, forgetting he did not somehow quite trust the man.

" When you have finished a film, let me have it to develop. You won't be able to get it done here. In a day or so my motor yacht will put in here, then you must get your parents' consent to make a short trip along the coast with me."

Before either could express excited approval of such a scheme, the Count explained he had voyaged all over the world, and occasionally wrote a history of some of the places he had visited.

Syre, he would have them believe, fascinated him, and if they could learn any interesting facts and legends, they were to tell him.

" I am particularly eager to learn the history of *the house* on the east cliff," he frankly admitted. " It's quite a modern house, possibly built on the site of an ancient one. That's a chance for you boys to prove how smart you are. I believe a boy of your own years lives there. I have heard so. It would be easy to make a friend of that boy and learn the history of *the house*. That is, of course, if you are interested in gaining knowledge."

Neither Noel nor Malcolm knew quite what to say. They averted their eyes from the smiling countenance of their generous friend, and were glad that the gloom hid their flaming cheeks.

" But I don't suppose you are really interested in a house, so don't worry," smiled the Count. " You have your boat, and there's swimming and playing at smugglers, which leaves very little time to bother about pleasing the fancy of an old man, who is anxious to write a history of Syre. History is dry stuff for young rascals to amuse themselves with."

The Count's English had improved remarkably since the launching.

He patted Noel on the shoulder, and remarked they must one day visit the old cottage that was once a smuggler's spy-place, and have a trip in his yacht.

" Well, sir," suggested Malcolm, feeling the Count deserved well of them. " You could go up to *the house* and ask about its history."

" I could," agreed the Count, smiling his rather twisted smile, and fingering his goaty beard. " But that would be rather rude. It's not quite the same thing for a couple of lively young rascals, playing at smugglers, to spy out the land. That is what smugglers should do."

He laughed as though he did not seriously mean them to spy, but the boys felt otherwise. They felt uneasy, and a little afraid of him.

Reminding them to bring the film to him when it was ready to be developed, he left them, saying he would take a stroll down to the harbour head.

Noel was too delighted with the gift to admit he did not like Count Aland. But Malcolm was too interested in the remarks of their strange friend to talk about anything else, as they strolled homeward.

"He must have seen Bertet!" breathed Malcolm.

"What does it matter?" asked Noel. "He can't know Bertet comes from *the house*. And, after all, as Count Aland writes about places, there is nothing strange that he should be curious to learn all about Syre."

"He hinted pretty pointedly that we should spy, Noel."

"The Count admitted frankly that he wanted us to find out all we could about *the house* and its history, Malcolm. And we're just as curious as he is, and tons luckier. We do know something."

Noel laughed.

"There is a frightfully good reason why Bertet is not allowed outside the gate," declared Malcolm.

"Can't see why that should worry us, Malcolm."

Malcolm said no more about the subject until they were undressing for bed, half an hour later.

"Noel, I don't believe the Count is interested in *the house* at all. He wants to find out who lives there."

"But he's not the only one, fathead," answered Noel, still under the influence of the camera. "Mr. Spanyard told us that some men came secretly one night, and a stranger was found unconscious under the wall next morning."

" Well, I vote we treat the Count as a Preventive man, anyway. Mr. Spanyard is different. He doesn't make me feel uneasy. As if he suspects what we know and wants us to talk, Noel."

Noel only laughed as he proudly examined the camera for the twentieth time, pointing out the automatic focusing gadget, and delayed action shutter action that would allow the photographer to appear in the picture.

The light out, Malcolm hesitated by the window. He could see the House of Golden Windows, now dark against the moon-flooded sky, and he dreamed about it that night.

Indeed, its influence seemed to be closing in upon them like a deepening and lengthening shadow, playing a more important part in their lives than they then realised. It kept its strange history to itself, and yet interweaving into their holiday a story yet to be told.

The House of Golden Windows was the first landmark to be seen on approaching Syre, and the last on leaving— either by land or sea. From the very first *the house* had fascinated them, and to the very end of their holidays it ruled them, drawing them nearer and nearer an adventure none was ever likely to forget, or tire in telling, even years hence.

CHAPTER IX

CAN'T BE A SMUGGLER

THE *Gallant* sailed from Syre next morning, all hands standing by and heavily armed for, as Fierce Fred remarked, and he ought to know what he was talking about, it was feared the Preventive men were vigilant.

It was rumoured—so he said before they sailed—that a company of dragoons were expected to arrive at Syre. Furthermore, Lively Lass reported that His Majesty's sloop *Thunder* was likely to make for the harbour.

Indeed, the " Devon Smugglers " had the hands of all

good citizens turned against them, though the taxes were not just and they gave generously to the poor.

Walnut Will had brought his camera. It had been proudly shown to old Mrs. Spraggart, who only remarked, quite crossly : " So the gentleman ought to give something after the way he ate and starved you all at the launching."

The wind was fretful, a hesitant breeze, that scarcely filled the sails so that, creeping beyond the harbour mouth, all hands were ordered to ship oars.

Kunning Kid caught a " crab ", and so violently did the good craft rock, as he crashed under the thwart, that she shipped a gallon or so of sea, not a little of it filling Lively Lass's wellington boots.

Old Mrs. Spraggart had bought a telescope from Exeter, which was Kunning Kid's proud possession, and, while gripping an oar with one hand, he kept on sweeping the sea with the toy, to catch a glimpse of His Majesty's sloop.

Fierce Fred and Walnut Will had received lanterns, while Lively Lass wore a pirate's hat with the skull and cross-bones on the broad upturned rim.

There was a haze over the water, and the heat was such that the male smugglers stripped to the buff, and soon found rowing more a task than a pleasure.

However, very gradually the coastline glided astern and the *Gallant* was " artfully conned through the shoal waters "—another expression of Fierce Fred's—into " Gory Cove ".

The craft was dragged through the shallow water to the bare wet sands. It was judged the tide would be in by the time they planned to depart during the afternoon.

Kunning Kid swept the cliffs and shores with his telescope for signs of the Preventive men, before Mrs. Spraggart's contraband was concealed in the cave, where the gloom and cooler atmosphere greatly restored them after a stormy and hazardous voyage through shark infested waters (Fierce Fred's imagination was particularly active).

The black interior of the cave did not attract Lively Lass, and as someone had to keep look-out against a surprise attack, she willingly undertook the duty.

It was also remembered that Spanish Main hoped to join them, in which event she was to whistle " Oranges and Lemons ", being the only tune she could whistle. As soon as the signal was heard, her companions were to return immediately from exploring the depth of the cave.

Lighting Mrs. Spraggart's anterns, the boys set off into the cave, Kunning Kid now and again glancing back rather longingly as the sunlight became dimmer and dimmer, and the mouth smaller and smaller.

They spoke in whispers, which came back to them in confused and mocking echoes, as though hundreds of invisible spies repeated every word they said, over and over again, each time fainter than the last.

When the entrance in their rear was no bigger than

a football, they discovered that the cave split into three branches, which was a very exciting discovery to make.

" Better not go any farther," advised Fierce Fred. " Our lanterns won't last long, and we ought to have thread to mark our passage, so we can't take the wrong turning and lose ourselves trying to get back."

Walnut Will agreed, partly because he had read it was easy to lose one's way in a cave that had branches, and also because he was feeling chilly, having omitted to slip on more clothing. Naked to the waist, his skin was " goose fleshed ".

" I expect it goes for miles and miles, a real smugglers' secret passage," whispered Fierce Fred. " I vote we search for treasure one day."

The suggestion thrilled Kunning Kid, who thought and said, with some hesitation, that their father should be invited to share the adventure with them, then it would be less easy to lose themselves, and that would save their mother from nights and nights of weeping before they would be found " as thin as skeletons ".

" Perhaps we ought, and, anyway, we can't explore today," answered Fierce Fred, as though he was not in the least afraid of going farther into the cave. " We must all swear to keep the secret."

Walnut Will could not resist in giving one mighty shout, that came back to them in dying echoes. Kunning Kid declared he could hear water trickling, and they held their breath, listening. He was impolitely told not to be "a little fathead" by Noel, for the ensuing silence was more frightening than the surrounding darkness.

Their return to the cave mouth was more bold and determined than their inward progress.

Spanish Main was there, with his wooden sword, but no other accoutrement of a "Devon Smuggler".

He was in high glee, and informed them that he had been given permission to remain alone in the wilderness of the garden until tea time, having been supplied with food and drink. That meant he could remain with them for some hours.

Quite naturally, and without protest from Fierce Fred, he took over command, and planned a game. Two were to be Preventive men, while the others were to run a rich contraband from Smite Cove to Headless Gap, the landmarks being two jutting ribs of white cliffs.

Fierce Fred and Walnut Will found themselves receiving orders, as eagerly as any. They marched off to conceal themselves amid the boulders, without even a protest.

For an hour that lonely beach rang with shouting and laughter, and blood-curdling cries, but always the smugglers won.

Tired by the midday heat, they became silent over lunch. During the rest, Fierce Fred realised he had allowed himself to be ordered about, and felt somewhat angry about it.

By this time, Spanish Main had succeeded in borrowing

two swords, three pistols, Fierce Fred's vivid shirt, one lantern, and Kunning Kid's telescope and, thus arrayed, had been photographed as chief of the Devon Smugglers.

Fierce Fred, brooding, made up his mind to assert himself during the afternoon. He had no intention of allowing Bertet Carlsen do all the bossing all the day.

Meanwhile, he sat somewhat apart from his cheerful comrades, feeling in the doldrums.

Long before another game was proposed, he regarded Spanish Main as a usurper, a prig, a stuck-up little swanker, much against the dictate of his conscience.

He was working himself into the mood to revolt, and thus regain the glory of his vanished leadership.

He wrote " fathead " and " prig " with his finger in the sand, and glanced stealthily at his comrades in the cave-mouth, hoping that they would see what he had written.

Spanish Main was very gay and full of laughter. Had he but realised how hurt Fierce Fred was feeling, he would have given up the leadership.

Gradually, the others ceased to talk, and only Spanish Main's voice reached the ears of the brooding Fierce Fred, reduced to one sword and minus his vivid shirt, on which he had inked the skull and cross-bones, quite omitting to realise that such was the symbol of bold, bad pirates.

Later, Spanish Main became pensive as he sat in the cave-mouth, with his chin resting on his drawn-up knees and hands clasped round his ankles. He did not speak of something that might happen, but as one convinced that what he said would come true.

One day, he told them, he would be a king and make his nation great, removing oppression, so that everyone would be free and happy.

He would keep a huge army and navy to be used in the cause of justice and peace, thus those nations he conquered, because they were brutal and warlike, would be free, their tyrannical rulers imprisoned.

Fierce Fred moved gradually closer to the party, much impressed and greatly envying the conviction with which Spanish Main spoke of his ambition.

Later, Walnut Will said it would be great fun if they could do some night smuggling. It would be easy to talk their parents into agreeing, but old Mrs. Spraggart was another problem. She was a stern and kindly tyrant, and believed that her "chicks" should go to roost by sunset.

Kunning Kid solved the problem.

"It'll soon be my birthday. Mrs. Spraggart always lets us have a favour on our birthday," he said. "If I ask her nicely, she'll agree."

"Good for you," cheered Walnut Will. "Mrs. Spraggart won't say no. After all, we can go to bed earlier the night before and, anyway, we needn't be so awfully late."

"Will you be able to come, Spanish Main?" asked Lively Lass. "It won't be fun without you."

"Sometimes, now that I am a big boy," answered Spanish Main, "I allowed am to go to bed late. Often it is I am let for to sleep in the garden. We must arrange plans so I join you, ja!"

Plans were necessary, so they discussed the idea in detail.

Spanish Main made a rough map in the sands, showing both east and west cliffs, with the harbour and deep valley between.

Fierce Fred listened to the plans for the night-smuggling, which were issued by Spanish Main, and felt a little sulky because their new friend seemed to be more popular than himself.

"I think it is a frightfully good idea," agreed Walnut Will, with enthusiasm, having listened to every detail with deep interest.

"I like the idea of signalling with lamps," exclaimed Lively Lass, for Spanish Main was to signal from the cliff-top (he took it for granted he would be able to lead the "running"—an expression used by the smugglers when contraband was to be shipped or landed), and Walnut Will was to reply from the harbour.

"Oars and rowlocks must be muffled, for the slightest sound will be heard by the Preventive men," whispered Kunning Kid, enthralled by the talk.

None took the least notice of Fierce Fred. He had turned his back upon them, and appeared to be dozing. He felt injured and left out, all because of his sulky mood.

He felt full of self-pity, and none noticed he was silent.

It was unnatural for him not to take the lead, and he was thinking how best he could do so without making a quarrel, which would spoil everything.

The worst of it was, which he had the good sense to realise, Spanish Main's plan was too good to be ignored. It was received by the others with such acclamation that the brooding rebel realised he could only regain his authority as leader by splitting the party. Then he could lead one side and Spanish Main the other.

He was quite sure his side would win !

" Don't you think it's a frightfully good idea ? " asked Walnut Will, giving Fierce Fred a hearty slap on the back. " It will be like a real running."

" Glad you think so," growled the fallen leader, frowning. " I don't ! I think it's rotten."

Spanish Main coloured, and his eyes looked angry. But he said nothing.

Lively Lass, who always felt sorry for anyone in the grumps, instantly played the part of a peacemaker by saying that it was a rule of the " Devon Smugglers " that each should have his say. They had done all the talking, and now Fierce Fred should be allowed to speak his mind.

" Well, so Fierce Fred can," protested Kunning Kid, whose sensitive nature sensed trouble. " But it's no good having a leader if we're all going to have our own way."

" In that case, I'd like to know since how long I haven't been leader ? " retorted Fierce Fred, reddening.

" Pleese, I am ver' sorry . . ." began Spanish Main, hurt that he had so innocently caused ill-feeling.

" Can't see why Fierce Fred should always be chief," interrupted Kunning Kid.

" Oh, I don't care, you ass," retorted Fierce Fred, caring very much indeed, and yet a little ashamed of his own ill-feeling. " All I think is that it is a rotten idea. I've the right to have my say. Spanish Main isn't English, so how can he know anything about ' Devon Smugglers ' ? "

" I haf made you ver' sorry with me," regretted Spanish Main. " Pleese, I do not und'stand."

" Oh, please, don't let us quarrel," pleaded Lively Lass, as the two would-be leaders glared at each other. " After all, we made our promise to Fierce Fred and . . ."

" Suppose we did ? " challenged Kunning Kid, gallantly standing up for his new friend. " Real smugglers change their leaders."

Walnut Will hesitated to take sides. He had always admired his chum and felt rather mean in not standing up openly for him now. He met the trouble half-way by saying : " I say, you lot, let's vote ! "

" All I can say is, Spanish Main's plan is rotten. I've got a better one. How can there be smugglers without Preventive men ? "

That was a clever remark. Fierce Fred aimed to split the forces, and to lead one side. He thought that that would be much better fun, and it would also give him a chance to prove he was the better leader of the pair.

" We must have Preventive men if we have smugglers," he insisted, as none answered. " And when we're not running a contraband, we'll all be smugglers together."

Lively Lass realised that Fierce Fred's suggestion would restore peace, and Walnut Will agreed because such an idea would make better fun. In other words, there was no real need for a quarrel.

" Pleese, you are right," said Spanish Main, offering his hand to Malcolm, which was readily accepted, for now Fierce Fred had spoken his mind, he felt friendly towards his rival. " Half a loaf is better than no bread ", so good spirits were restored, and they gathered eagerly around Fierce Fred as he outlined his plan.

" The smugglers will sail from the harbour, and the Preventive men must try to stop them from landing and placing their contraband in the cave," he said, happy once again. " Anyone losing their life must run to the cave and get another. We must all wear a paper streamer, and once that is torn off, we're dead until we get another."

" Spiffing idea," voiced Walnut Will. " But no Preventive man may attack within one hundred yards of the cave."

" Of course not," agreed Fierce Fred. " Spanish Main will lead the Preventive men."

" Pleese, I want for to not do that. I am a smuggler."

" Some of us must be Preventive men," argued Fierce Fred. " Lively Lass and Kunning Kid can be your followers. That's fair, as we two are a bit older."

" But, pleese, why not you be Preventive men ? "

Spanish Main rather fancied himself in Fierce Fred's bright shirt, and was proud of his even gaudier sash bristling with small arms.

" So I could be, Spanish Main. But after you talking about wanting to be a great king, how can you be a smuggler ? Smugglers are the enemy of the king. After all, if you really want to be a king one day, you must behave like a king now. Stands to reason, doesn't it ? "

Spanish Main drew himself up proudly. There was a moment of embarrassing silence, for the Strathmore children did not wish to favour either Spanish Main or Fierce Fred.

" If you really want to be a king, you must really hate smugglers," argued Fierce Fred.

" Pleese, why do smugglers hate the king ? "

" If you don't know that," cried Fierce Fred, triumph- antly, " you're no smuggler at heart. They don't really hate the king, but the taxes that are not just, and the poor have to live. It is the king's ministers who are to blame. The ' Devon Smugglers ' are valiant fighters for the king when war comes."

" Ja, I und'stand. Then you be the smugglers . . ."

" Only for this one night," Fierce Fred hastened to explain, feeling he mustn't be unfair. " Then we can change, or all be smugglers again. I say, everything is arranged. Kunning Kid has only to get Mrs. Spraggart to agree, and she's a ripping sport."

But when the plans were finally arranged for the great night, and the boys had had a swim, it was time to sail away in the *Gallant*, that was now afloat on the incoming tide.

Spanish Main returned the shirt and weapons he had borrowed from his friends.

After the swim, Fierce Fred sauntered alone amid the big boulders close to the cave-mouth. He made a startling discovery which he kept to himself, not wishing to alarm Gwen and Dudley.

He was in a quiet and anxious mood when he rejoined his friends, and said " good-bye " to Spanish Main in a spirit of greater friendliness.

Kunning Kid was only too pleased to follow Spanish Main's lead, while Lively Lass always agreed with what others wanted to do. Walnut Will felt that somehow Fierce Fred would continue to be jealous of Spanish Main who, in his turn, was imperious and rather over-eager to be the leader all the time.

There was a light breeze, and the ship's progress was sluggish. Fierce Fred did not stand on the for'ard half-deck, sweeping the horizon for His Majesty's sloop of war, but brooded in the stern, as though sorely troubled.

" Hope you're not going to spoil the fun, Malcolm, by

sulking," Noel remarked, a little impatiently. " Can't see why you should'nt take a back seat for once. "

" Hang it all, man, Bertet's a newcomer and wants to boss the show," answered Malcolm. " I admit he's frightfully decent, but you can't deny he's got too much side. Anyway, I'm not worrying about him."

" He's a born leader," answered Noel. " He behaved decently, though you were frightfully rude. After all, Malcolm, just because I've let you do the bossing, you can't expect a chap like Bertet to agree always."

Malcolm (for neither had a thought about smuggling during their first quarrel) pouted, and he looked defiantly at his chum. He was a good-looking, strong-willed youngster, whose vanity slightly smarted.

" What do you mean by ' a chap like Bertet ' ? He is our age and perhaps can swim, box, and play cricket as good as we can. But he's nothing out of the way."

Malcolm's voice sounded rather angry.

" He's different, somehow, that's all," answered Noel. " Some chaps are born to rule and, perhaps, he has the right to do so. When he spoke this afternoon of wanting to be a king, he spoke as though he really meant it, and had the right to be one."

" Yes, he did," agreed Malcolm, in a more pleasant voice. " I'm sorry if I have been a rotten prig. I'll apologise to Bertet when I next see him. If the ' Devon Smugglers ' like to vote him their leader, I'll be decent about it."

"Thanks, you can be a pretty decent sport when you care, Malcolm."

Noel realised that the offer was both generous and sincere, and that it cost his friend an effort, for Malcolm at school even was always the leader.

"Bertet's the first chap I felt I could follow. At least, I didn't feel that way this afternoon, but I do now," assured Malcolm, pleasantly. "I know he will always get the better of me. That's why I suggested having Preventive men. I wanted to show him I can lead and win. I suppose it was a bit mean of me."

They became silent as the harbour mouth was approached.

On entering "home waters", Malcolm Brewster became Fierce Fred again, and roared orders as he waved his sword, much to the admiration of several children on the harbour wall.

His crew of bold "Devon Smugglers" leapt to their posts as the *Gallant* crept to her berth, in the brilliant glare of the westering sun.

CHAPTER X

'WARE SPY !

THE *Gallant* was made snug for the night. As soon as the excitement of landing was over, Fierce Fred became silent and mentally occupied again.

He lagged behind the others as they strolled along the cobbled street homeward and, close to where the nets were drying, signalled to Walnut Will to let Lively Lass and Kunning Kid get ahead.

The younger pair were chattering about the proposed night smuggling too eagerly to notice the elder boys were not following.

" I say, Noel, I don't want to alarm the kids, but I believe someone spied on us down at the cave."

" You're being honest and not larking ? " asked Noel, startled.

" Honest Injun. After our swim, I sauntered on my own and saw an impression of a body in the sand behind some boulders, quite close to the cave-mouth.

" Someone had lain there. The big boulder at the entrance to the cave hid us. I don't suppose we were seen, but they must have heard what we said. Whoever it was must have gone before we went for a swim."

" I didn't see anyone approach along the beach, Malcolm. Sure you're right ? "

Noel felt rather alarmed.

" The full tide covers the spot, so the person must have lain there after we arrived," said Malcolm, gravely. " From where we sat in the cave-mouth, we wouldn't have seen anyone approaching along the beach, Noel. It's up to you and me to keep our eyes skinned in the future."

Noel crossed to the harbour wall, and sat on it.

He felt that the matter deserved serious thought and discussion.

" I can't see why anyone should want to spy on us ! "

" I've been thinking about it," Malcolm answered, frowning. " It's not us they were spying on, but Bertet. He isn't really allowed to leave the garden, and there must be a good reason. There is something more than strange going on, Noel, and I don't think I quite like it·

Bertet doesn't say anything about himself. There is a mystery somewhere, and we've got to get to the bottom of it."

" Are you sure the impression in the sand was that of a man ? " asked Noel.

" It was that of a tall person, and even the buttons of the jacket were clear," whispered Malcolm. " None of the local inhabitants would spy on us. They don't seem in the least bit interested in us. But there is Mr. Spanyard, Noel.

" After all, why is he hovering around here ? He seems to be an educated man and there can't be anything to attract him in this dump of a place, yet he stays here."

Noel felt troubled. The shadow of *the house*, and its strange history, was creeping over them, but they did not know that.

" We can't very well do anything at the present," Malcolm continued, in a whisper. " But as we can't be of interest to anyone, it must be Bertet who was spied on. We ought to warn him at the first chance, but it's no good scaring Gwen and Dudley."

" Perhaps I had better say something to father," suggested Noel.

" It's no good saying anything until we're sure we know what we are talking about," Malcolm warned his chum. " We could try to find out whether Mr. Spanyard has been along the beach today."

Noel nodded.

He glanced thoughtfully towards the harbour mouth. A sharp cry burst from his lips as he pointed in the direction in which he stared so fixedly.

There, across the water caught in the lowering sun, a magnificent yacht was creeping in. She was white, as lovely a ship as ever they had seen. She looked frail and beautiful.

From across the water came the clatter of anchor links leaping through the hawse-pipe. The plunging anchor threw up a fountain of sparkling spray, awaking echoes off the little cottages.

The inhabitants of Syre crowded into the cobbled street, as though some secret and pre-arranged signal had been given. They expressed no excitement, but gravely regarded the ship stolidly, without betraying any emotion.

Here and there the eyes of some of the watchers glimmered morosely, as once their sires undoubtedly had when watching a man-o'-war anchor in the harbour, which meant for a time an end to their smuggling and ship-wrecking activities.

Malcolm and Noel watched davits being swung out, and a boat was lowered ; a boat as white and sun-bright as the ship herself. The crew were in spotless white ; fine, strapping men of rather sallow complexions, and sharp features.

Foreigners !

" A fine ship, is she not ? "

The voice was suave and familiar. They turned to find

Count Aland standing behind them, smiling a smile that was not pleasing.

" I trust you will permit me the honour of taking you both aboard my yacht before many days are past," he said, in a voice that had a tinge of pride and boastfulness.

Malcolm frankly gulped.

" Your yacht, sir ! " exclaimed Noel, finding his voice after a moment of stupefaction.

" The yacht in which I promised to give you a short voyage," answered the Count. " Of course, with the permission of your father. But, come, I am in haste now and can only invite you to accompany me in the dinghy. Later, another time, you must be my guests aboard."

Count Aland turned, hesitated to light a cigarette, his sharp sloe-like eyes fixed upon Mr. Spanyard standing in the doorway of his cottage.

A slow, artful smile spread over the Count's sallow features, for he had overheard part of the chum's conversation before he had joined them.

" A strange man, is Mr. Spanyard," he remarked, with an indifferent shrug of his narrow shoulders. " Very fond of roaming alone along the beach towards Earlie Cove. I wonder what he finds there to interest him."

The boys exchanged rapid glances. The cunning, evil words had reached their mark.

" I am remaining here a few days, and will make it my business to know Mr. Spanyard," declared the Count,

" Perhaps he would tell me something interesting about the history of *the house*."

Noel and Malcolm instinctively glanced towards the House of Golden Windows that looked mellow in the flood of sunlight, its windows tinted, but not as yet flashing like sheets of burnished gold.

" My little history notes of Syre is incomplete, my young friends, and that is to be regretted," smiled the Count.

" However, you should take a photograph of my ship now. The water looks quite golden and her reflection is perfect."

" I have only one exposure left, sir."

" Then take a picture of my ship, and give me the film to have developed," suggested the Count. " Tomorrow, you shall have the prints."

The inhabitants, who had gathered along the quay, parted to allow the Count and the two boys to descend the stairway and reach the dinghy alongside. Oars were raised in salute, and the officer in command stood as though in welcome.

Seated, the Count gave some order in a foreign tongue, and set out for the yacht. He ordered the boat to hove to, in order to allow Noel to take a photograph.

" It is too late to detain you now," suggested the Count, as the dinghy drew alongside the ship, and the Count prepared to mount the Jacob's ladder. " I will take your film if you wish."

Noel handed him the film.

It was clear to both the boys that the Count did not desire their company any longer that evening. They were too late for tea, but had some time to spare before supper.

Both glanced enviously in the direction of the yacht, as they were taken shoreward, disappointed that they had not been allowed to board her.

Before ascending the Jacob's ladder, the Count had glanced shoreward, and the chums followed the direction of his glance. There, on the harbour wall, stood Mr. Spanyard, with his model of a windjammer, seeming not in the least interested in the white steam yacht that had attracted so much attention.

" A strange man is Mr. Spanyard," the Count commented. " I am curious by nature and must get to know him better. By his speech, I would say he is not a native of these parts."

" No, sir," answered Noel. " Mr. Spanyard is very clever, and has made a wonderful model of a ship. He was kind enough to step a new mast to our boat so that she could carry sail."

" A friend of yours, eh ! " smiled the Count. " It is a pity I am so curious. I thought I saw him wandering along the beach towards Earlie Cove this afternoon. Perhaps, however, I was wrong. It would be interesting to know what could attract such a man to remain here."

" On holiday, I suppose, sir," suggested Malcolm, feeling a little irritated by Count Aland's comments. " He is our friend and we like him very much."

Noel elbowed his chum in the ribs to keep quiet, for the remark seemed to displease the Count for, though he smiled, the next moment he frowned for an instant.

" I envy Mr. Spanyard such a privilege," the Count told the chums, with a heartiness that was not altogether sincere. " I hope that when we come to know each other better I may have the pleasure of your friendship. Permit me to suggest that you should not allow your friendship for Mr. Spanyard to encourage too much confidence."

" Can't see why we should suspect him, sir," rather sharply from the ever-ready to-say-what-he-thought Malcolm Brewster. "Anyway, he's not out to gain anything by being friendly. There is nothing to gain ! "

" Perhaps I am over-anxious on your behalf, my young friends," answered the Count, in a casual manner. " But I feel . . . yes, feel instinctively that Mr. Spanyard is here for a reason that may lead to trouble. You see, I have placed my confidence in you. I may be wrong. I hope I am, but I prefer to warn you than to remain silent and regret it later."

The two boys remained silent.

" When did Mr. Spanyard come here ? " asked the Count.

" I believe it was about the same time as when *the house* was occupied," blurted out Noel. " Mr. Spanyard said so."

" Ah ! But perhaps Mr. Spanyard, like myself, is very interested in strange houses and ancient places."

" Mr. Spanyard told us that a spy lived there years ago. That was before the Great War of 1914. And that one night . . ."

Noel stopped, for his chum had jogged him in the ribs, and had scowled warningly. Noel could see no reason for being secretive, but Malcolm apparently had a good reason to discourage confiding too much in Count Aland.

" But that was one night . . . what ? " asked Count Aland, still standing on the bottom rung of the Jacob's ladder.

" Oh, nothing much, sir," answered the embarrassed and flushing Noel Strathmore. " We were talking one evening and Mr. Spanyard said that one morning a man was found unconscious close to the wall of *the house*."

" A man was found at dawn, my young friend," corrected Count Aland. " The story remains current hereabouts. It is no secret. It was quite an event for this sleepy place. They have so little to excite their lives. That sad-looking house," he remarked, glancing towards the east cliff, " seems to brood over this lovely place, casting its influence upon it, an influence that makes me feel uneasy. Indeed, I have not even been near *the house*. I would prefer not ! "

Noel held his tongue, catching a warning glance from his chum. The Count, finding neither answered, bade them " good-night " and promised an early invitation to visit the yacht.

Without a word of command, for the officer had

E

followed his master up the Jacob's ladder, the boat was rowed back to the steps. In silence, the chums watched the boat cut through the placid waters, after they had landed, and be raised and swung inboard.

"There is something about Count Aland I don't like," remarked Malcolm. "I feel he wants to make use of us."

"I don't feel that way, I think he is just curious," Noel answered, too frank and open by nature to think ill of anyone with whom he came in contact.

Malcolm had a mind no less honest, but more shrewd. Mentally, he was older, something of a schemer without knowing it, otherwise he would never have thought of Preventive men in order to regain something of his lost leadership. "In fact, Malcolm, he quite frankly told us he was curious."

"That house," gravely from Malcolm, ignoring the comment, glancing towards the east cliff, "seems to be drawing us into some kind of adventure. It was the first of Syre we saw, and somehow we can't escape from it."

"You're getting romantic, Malcolm," laughed Noel. "And you don't like Count Aland because he is a foreigner. Jolly sporting of him to have given me a camera, anyway."

"He can't really be so interested in chaps our age unless he has a good reason, Noel," warned Malcolm, feeling older and superior. "Each time he has spoken to us he talks of *the house*, as though he suspects we could say more than we admit to."

" So we could say more than we do," admitted Noel, light-heartedly. " The Count admits he's here to find out all he can about Syre and that house."

They strolled homeward in silence.

Mr. Spanyard was not by the harbour wall as they passed along the cobbled street.

Malcolm thought deeply over what the Count had said, and his words were slowly taking effect upon his mind.

" You're right, Noel ! The Count is quite frank about being curious. Somehow, too frank for my liking ! "

The two elder boys would have an hour or more to spare after supper. No sooner was the meal over and Dudley had gone off to bed, than Malcolm proposed they should go down to the harbour and muffle the oars and rowlocks of the *Gallant*, in preparation for the proposed night smuggling on Dudley's birthday.

They had eagerly chattered about the subject during supper, hoping to impress old Mrs. Spraggart.

Dudley's birthday was two days ahead, but preparations for their game were begun without delay, for the next morning Mrs. Spraggart was going shopping, to Exeter by car, with Mrs. Strathmore, and Gwen was to go with them, carrying commissions from Malcolm and Noel, in addition to buying her own birthday present for her younger brother.

Noel and Malcolm planned having the next day to themselves, voting that they would give smuggling a rest.

CHAPTER XI

THE WARNING

MALCOLM and Noel required quite a lot of old clothes, pieces of flannel, and string for muffling the oars and rowlocks of the *Gallant*.

Mrs. Spraggart, when she was consulted about the problem said " Drat ! Can't a body ever have any rest ? " and immediately searched and supplied them with the necessities, obviously quite pleased to do so, and curious to know the why and wherefore, which the boys hoped, in readily explaining, would " break the ice " for Dudley who was to ask for the favour of a really late night on his birthday.

Malcolm explained why they required such oddments, but Mrs. Spraggart pretended not to be really interested, beyond finding some cloth. She sniffed quite a lot and said : " Stuff and nonsense ". Noel considered such to be a good sign, for the dear old soul generally pretended to be cross before granting a favour.

" Mrs. S. didn't seem very patient with us, Noel. Perhaps it would have been better if I'd explained everything," remarked Malcolm, as they set off for the harbour shortly after supper.

" Oh, don't worry," assured Noel. " Mrs. Spraggart always pretends to be cross. When Dud asks her point-blank for a birthday favour, she'll look surprised and ' hum ' and ' hah ', and make a lot of fuss and bother, then later agree to have peace of mind, so she'll say. She's a real sporting old dear, Malcolm, but can be difficult if she is really angry. We've got to be careful not to anger her, that's all."

They strolled towards the harbour.

The shadows were lengthening now, and it was very still, as though nature was settling down to sleep.

The white yacht in the harbour looked vivid in the glare of the setting sun.

They saw Mr. Spanyard sitting in the doorway of his cottage, smoking. His presence was indistinct from up the road, but the glow of his pipe forewarned them that their friend was at home.

" There's Mr. Spanyard. He'll want to know what

we're going to do with all this stuff, Malcolm."

"It's not his business," answered Malcolm. "Anyway, we needn't make a frightful secret that we're going to play smuggling at night. If he begins asking questions about us, there are a few we could ask him about himself. And I might tell him so."

"You mean, about spying on us this afternoon?" asked Noel, somewhat alarmed.

"Well, yes," admitted Malcolm, stoutly. "He had no right to do that. Frightfully mean thing to have done, and I've half a mind to tell Mr. Spanyard so. I'm not scared of him, Noel."

"Better go steady, Malcolm. We're not really sure that he did spy on us, you know."

"Anyway, who else would have?"

On nearing the cottage, Mr. Spanyard gave a welcoming shout, and invited them to have a cup of coffee he had just made. The boys declined the offer, but crossed the street to have a few words with him.

Malcolm felt it would be as well to let Mr. Spanyard know they suspected him of spying.

"What's in the wind now, my hearties?" asked Mr. Spanyard, eyeing their bundles.

He was dressed in old white trousers and a singlet that left bare his thick, muscular arms. His chest was powerful, and Malcolm felt the man was strong enough to give a very good account of himself if the need arose.

"We're going to muffle the oars and rowlocks of the

Gallant, Mr. Spanyard," explained Noel, frankly. " We're hoping to play at night smuggling on Dudley's birthday. Mustn't make a sound, you know. Smugglers always muffle their oars and rowlocks."

Mr. Spanyard removed his pipe, sent a stream of tobacco smoke into the air, and frowned.

" Better abed, in my opinion," his voice sounded gruff and displeased. " Easy enough to have an accident when it's dark. Nice ado if you chaps capsize the boat."

" We can all swim," answered Malcolm, who quite rightly felt that Mr. Spanyard would discourage their enterprise. " Anyway, we shan't be far off shore and it'll be fun."

" Maybe, but seems to me you would be better abed. What night have you chosen ? "

" Dudley's birthday, night after tomorrow, Mr. Spanyard," Noel answered.

The man appeared to be uneasy, fidgeting and frowning, clearly disapproving, but not minded to express his thoughts too frankly.

" Why not later on ? " he asked. " Say at the end of the month. Perhaps by then I could get some local boys to join in. They could be Preventive men."

" We've got Preventive men, sir," explained Noel. " And I don't think we want the local boys. You see, it's Dudley's birthday the day after tomorrow, and Mrs. Spraggart is almost sure to let us have a birthday favour. Besides," triumphantly pointed out Noel, " we don't want more than three Preventive men and two smugglers. Malcolm and me are to be the smugglers. It's all planned."

"Three Preventive men!" remarked Mr. Spanyard, surprised. "And two smugglers. I thought there were only four of you altogether."

Too late, Noel realised his mistake and felt uneasy. It would never do to mention Bertet Carlsen. Malcolm was irritated by the man's obvious desire to discourage the plan.

"Well, there are five of us now," he answered, sharply. "And I can't see why you should want to stop us, Mr. Spanyard. We can't do any harm to anyone, and we shan't be allowed to be so frightfully late."

"I've no right to stop you. It's not really my business," admitted Mr. Spanyard, quite pleasantly. "But I do think it would be much better fun if some of the local boys joined in."

"We don't want them to," answered Malcolm, bluntly.

"But it would be awfully thrilling to have a mob," suggested Noel, anxious in case his chum should speak his mind too frankly and offend Mr. Spanyard.

"You know as well as I do, Noel, that Mrs. Spraggart will only give permission as a birthday favour, if she gives it at all," said Malcolm, crossly. "There is no time to alter the plans now, and it's useless to talk about a later date."

Malcolm resented the attempt to interfere.

" I don't know who Mrs. Spraggart is, but if she's likely . . ."

" You met her at the launching, sir," said Noel, astonished and perhaps a little hurt that such a generous, fussing old body should have been so soon forgotten.

" Oh, yes, of course I know Mrs. Spraggart, " admitted Mr. Spanyard. " You seem to be sure she will give permission, so why not make a later date and we all can join in? I'd like to myself, but I couldn't for a night or so."

" We'd like you to join in, Mr. Spanyard. It would be ripping fun," agreed Noel, but Malcolm frowned, for he had not forgotten that Count Aland had seen Mr. Spanyard strolling along the beach that afternoon, and that he was probably the person who had spied on them.

" I'd like to know, Mr. Spanyard, why you should want to spy on us this afternoon ? " he asked.

Mr. Spanyard did not seem to be offended, and Noel was more than surprised that he did not become angry. Noel felt most uneasy and not a little cross with his friend.

" What makes you think that ? " the man asked, calmly. Indeed, he was most friendly towards them.

" I happen to know you were along the beach this afternoon and as somebody spied on us . . ."

" Naturally, I am the culprit ! Admittedly, none of the local folk would trouble to take interest in what you boys get up to," agreed Mr. Spanyard. " I did not tell you I was along the beach. I was, however ! "

Malcolm flushed, but remained stubborn.

Noel hastily suggested they should go down to the boat, but Mr. Spanyard was not prepared to allow the matter to drop.

For once, he looked grim and angry.

" I have the right to know who told you I was along the beach this afternoon," he said. " There is nothing extraordinary in that ! "

" Well, sir, you've admitted it," retorted Malcolm, puzzled why Mr. Spanyard had tried to discourage their smuggling plans for the night of Dudley's birthday.

"I do not intend either to deny or admit the accusation, Malcolm," was the frank and not unfriendly answer. " I do not consider that I am called upon to account for my movements. I will ask you a question, but you are at liberty not to answer. Did you see me along the beach, spying on you ? "

" I didn't say that, sir," answered Malcolm, uneasily. " Someone spied and, as we were told you were along the beach, I . . . Well, I thought you to be the most likely person. Perhaps that seems a bit unsporting."

" Well, your power of reasoning is certainly more praiseworthy than your manners, my boy," answered Mr. Spanyard, rather coolly. " Perhaps Count Aland saw me. You appear to be very friendly with him, and quite certain that I was along the beach this afternoon."

Malcolm refused to answer.

" Why should I spy ? " demanded Mr. Spanyard.

"You seem to suspect me and must have some idea why I should spy on you boys."

"That's rather difficult to say, sir," admitted Malcolm, more angry with himself than resentful towards the suspect. "You might have been anxious to find out who our fifth member was."

"I didn't happen to know you had a fifth member until you said so a few moments ago," answered Mr. Spanyard. "And if you had fifty-five members, I doubt whether I would be particularly interested."

"Anyway, I seem to be wrong, Mr. Spanyard. I'm sorry," apologised Malcolm. "Someone spied and we don't like it. We're doing no harm, sir. You . . . Well, you haven't denied it, anyway."

"Perhaps you may be doing a lot of harm," answered Mr. Spanyard, gravely, ignoring the comment. "And running into danger. I've no doubt you were spied on, but I would have thought I was the last person you would have picked on ! Perhaps you would like to know why I am here. Curious, eh ? "

Malcolm did not answer.

Noel felt that it was his duty to be loyal to his chum, and greatly admired him for facing Mr. Spanyard so boldly, an attitude more honourable, perhaps, though ill-mannered, than keeping such a suspicion to themselves.

"Come, come, you must have wondered what I am doing here," urged Mr. Spanyard, who certainly had lost his genial mood.

" Well, yes, we have wondered that, sir," admitted Malcolm. " Strangers aren't made welcome here, and you don't seem to have anything in particular to do. It's frightfully quiet here."

" Did anyone put such ideas into your heads ? "

"Never mind that, sir," answered Malcolm. "You haven't denied you spied, sir, and I can't think who else."

" I like your frankness," admitted Mr. Spanyard. " There's Count Aland, also a stranger here, but who seems to have a very good reason for coming. He's writing a book about Syre, and also another about the strange houses of England. I've no doubt you are good friends of his, and I'll say no more."

Mr. Spanyard knocked out his pipe against the door-post, and sparks drifted to the ground.

" Malcolm, I hope we will remain friends," he added, after a moment's pause. " I like your honesty. Trust me for the time being. I'm your friend, that was why I said I didn't want you to go night smuggling. It may prove to be more dangerous than you think."

Malcolm was stubborn : " It's mean to spy, sir."

" Some men have to spy for a very good reason," said Mr. Spanyard. " Tell me, does your friend, the Count, want you to help him in his work ? He's interested in *the house* on the east cliff, and so are you boys."

" He only asked what we knew about *the house*, sir," admitted Noel. " I'm awfully sorry if you're offended, but Malcolm thought it was more decent to ask you to your face rather than suspect you."

"Point is, Mr. Spanyard, you haven't denied it," protested Malcolm, setting his lips grimly.

"I fancy you're not saying what you really suspect, but what Count Aland has put into your heads," answered Mr. Spanyard. "Have you, Malcolm—since you're doing so much of the talking—asked him why he should pick upon an unknown place like Syre for a visit? It's scarcely worth writing about. He's travelled all over the world and could as easily visit a dozen places far more interesting?"

"I can't see what that has to do with the argument, sir," protested Malcolm. "You don't seem to approve of our night smuggling . . ."

"Oh, well, Malcolm, let's say no more," urged Noel, uneasily.

"Your chum is honest and downright, and that isn't a crime," Mr. Spanyard interrupted, quietly. "I only suggest that if you want to play at night smuggling, why not wait and plan a really big affair? The local boys would enjoy it, and it would be much better fun. However, we do not seem to be the best of friends tonight. Did you tell your friend, Count Aland, about your plans?"

"We might have said something, sir," admitted Noel. "Can't remember, really."

"He didn't discourage you?"

"No, sir, not as far as I can remember," answered Noel.

" Well, go ahead, my boys. If ever you feel in need of a friend, remember I shall always welcome you and do what I can. Goodnight ! "

Mr. Spanyard turned and went within doors.

The two boys sauntered down to their boat, feeling uneasy and dispirited. Noel very much regretted the incident.

" Anyway, he didn't deny he had spied on us," said Malcolm, stubbornly. " And I don't think anyone else would have. And it wasn't what he said, but how he said it. He was cold and off-handed, sneering at me all the time."

" I didn't think so. Anyway, you couldn't expect him to like what you said," answered Noel.

Malcolm did not answer.

They set to work to muffle oars and rowlocks, working in silence. Malcolm sulked a little, which he sometimes did when he felt opposed by Noel. But very soon recovered his usual light spirits.

Now the windows of *the house* on the east cliff were flashing in the sunlight, and the white yacht was tinted a pale golden hue. There was no sign of life aboard, and the harbour itself was devoid of other human beings.

It was almost like being in a strange world of their own.

" Mr. Spanyard was frightfully annoyed with you, Malcolm," said Noel, suddenly, his mind still worried. " He's been ripping towards us, and offered to help us whenever we like to ask him."

" I know about all that, Noel. But you're a bit of a simpleton. I'm not letting him think we're a trusting lot of babes, anyway ! "

" I know you meant frightfully well. And I don't suppose he really minds very much," answered Noel.

Malcolm completed muffling an oar before he spoke again.

" It's not for him to mind. We've the right to find out who spied on us. Only two persons could have, Noel. I don't like Count Aland somehow, but he hasn't been secretive about himself like Mr. Spanyard has. And he isn't so grown-up and superior towards us as Mr. Spanyard was tonight."

Noel did not answer.

They worked steadily in silence, and at the end of half an hour their tasks were finished.

It was time for them to return home.

Malcolm was again his usual bright self, full of great schemes of how they would outwit the Preventive men. He had spoken his mind and felt all the better. It was not his nature to suppress his impulsive thoughts always.

" By the way, Noel," he remarked, as they made the boat snug for the night, " you put your foot into it, so you needn't talk about me. Mr. Spanyard will try to find out who our third Preventive man is. Didn't you notice he gave quite a start when you admitted five of us were going to play night smuggling ? "

" Can't see why a simple remark like that should have startled him, Malcolm."

"Well, it did ! And I suppose because he is sure we haven't made friends with any of the local boys. I do believe he suspects the fifth is from *the house*."

Noel whistled a note of surprise : " I was a silly ass, Malcolm. But if he spied, he already knows we have found a friend in Bertet."

"The boulder hid the cave-mouth so he could only have heard voices. I do wish I knew why he wanted to spy on us ? "

"Malcolm, we've forgotten one thing," pointed out Noel, gravely. There was a note of triumph in his voice. ' You saw Count Aland spying in the garden. It's the Count who is keen for us to find out all we can about *the house*. Perhaps he is the spy after all ? "

Malcolm did not agree. For one thing, Count Aland had not concealed that he was anxious to learn the history of *the house*, and he had made no secret why he had come to Syre. Furthermore, he had admitted that he had been in Mr. Strathmore's garden on the evening in question the evening when Bertet Carlsen had visited them.

"Malcolm, come to think of it, he hid behind a bush and talked about finding a bird's nest. Sounds a bit queer ! "

"Anyway, he was honest about it, Noel. Mr. Spanyard isn't so frank with us ! "

Noel was impressed by his friend's argument. But Mr. Spanyard's kindness to them urged his conscience to dispute his chum's conviction that he was right in suspecting Mr. Spanyard. However, he said nothing.

Later, as they passed up the shadowy drive, something white fell at their feet. It was a piece of paper wrapped round a stone. Unfolding it and smoothing out the wrinkled sheet, they saw a message written in pencil.

" IT MAY BE DANGEROUS TO PLAY SMUGGLERS AT NIGHT."

" It's a warning, Malcolm," exclaimed the startled Noel. " What do you think ? "

" If Mr. Spanyard thinks he can frighten me, he can't ! How can there be danger, anyway ? "

" But it may not be from Mr. Spanyard," suggested Noel. " I am sure he wouldn't want to scare us, Malcolm. He tried to discourage the idea. Perhaps someone is trying to be funny."

" But who else knows about our plans ? " asked Malcolm. " Only Mr. Spanyard, and you said something or other about it to the Count, as we were rowed to the yacht. Can't be any of the folks here."

" Someone might have overheard us this evening, or watched us muffling the oars," suggested Noel, unwilling to suspect either Count Aland or Mr. Spanyard. " Voices travel so on a still evening, you know."

Malcolm was far too thrilled by the thought, that perhaps there was danger in night smuggling, to wish to ignore the warning. In his heart, he believed that someone was trying to tease rather than frighten them, but he gave his chum the impression there was a real mystery in which they were somehow involved.

His imaginative mind fancied all kinds of dangers, and his eager talk left Noel feeling uneasy.

Even when they were in bed, and the only light was the pale moon outside of their bedroom window, Malcolm persisted in his belief that the warning was no hoax.

Noel felt thrilled and anxious, anxious especially for Gwen and Dudley.

" I don't mind the risk, Malcolm, but it's different with Gwen and my kid brother."

" Oh, we'll look after them. They'll be all right," answered Malcolm. " Anyway, they'll be on land as Preventive men. It's Mr. Spanyard seeing whether he can frighten you and me from going out in the boat. We'll say nothing about the warning, or we shan't be allowed the favour. You're not really scared, are you, Noel ? "

" 'Course not," whispered Noel, in a doubtful tone of voice. " It's only some silly ass trying to be funny. I say, it's going to be frightfully thrilling."

" You can bet it will be," agreed Malcolm. " Good-night, old man ! "

The shadows deepened, and the dim light beyond the window faded.

The full tide was very quiet. Ceaseless time was marching on, soon to reveal the mystery of *the house*, and perhaps, too, was bearing the Devon Smugglers on the adventure that was to be no happy and care-free make-believe.

CHAPTER XII

MYSTERIOUS MESSAGE

NEXT morning was warm and windless. The heat-wave was likely to continue for many days, so said Mr. Strathmore, who was no weather prophet.

Noel was awake early and, from his bedroom window, he could see the white yacht of Count Aland, looking rather ghostly through the mist that was rapidly clearing. He pulled the clothes off his chum's bed, and shook him into wakefulness, then he proposed a swim down at the harbour.

Neither gave a thought to recent events.

They did not even think of the warning!

Here was another glorious day before them, full of sunlight and adventure.

Waving their towels, they ran down the drive to the sea, their naked feet pitter-pattering, and echoing softly off the cottages.

Smoke climbed lazily from many chimneys and, down at the harbour, fishermen were spreading their nets out to dry, after a night of toil. Old men and young— brawny, bronzed and daring they mostly looked—worked without haste, as though time could not assail them. One sang in a deep, powerful voice, a sailor's song of the sea, of storm and stress and of a lass awaiting the boat's return to harbour.

The two friends had watched such an early scene before, and paused now, but none took any notice of them.

There was a strong smell of fish on the morning air, and the tap, tap, tap of hammers accompanied the singer as box lids were nailed down and loaded into a waiting lorry, that was to carry a varied supply of fish to the cities and towns inland.

After their swim, they returned home for breakfast, aching with hunger, to find Gwen " dressed in her best ", and somewhat excited about her shopping expedition with old Mrs. Spraggart.

A whispered conference followed between Gwen, Malcolm and Noel, which Dudley was not permitted to overhear. Gwen was to buy birthday presents, and they

were to be hidden on her return so that Dudley would not find them by accident.

Old Mrs. Spraggart was seen trotting between the breakfast-room and kitchen, her greying hair in paper curlers, fussing and fuming as though about to set off on a dangerous mission, far into the back o' beyond.

Mr. Strathmore was busy seeing to the car, which his wife was to drive. One thing and another, it almost seemed as though the entire household was preparing to see the three voyagers off with little prospect of seeing them for ages.

Noel's weekly story paper arrived by post, also some mysterious parcels for " Master Dudley ", which were breathlessly whisked away by Mrs. Spraggart before Dudley could even tell the colour of the wrappings, or make a guess at the contents.

" Tomorrow, my chick ! "

Mrs. Spraggart's " chick " watched her vanish, well-laden, and as important as a Cabinet Minister running away to hide a state secret from a horde of spies.

In the weekly story paper Noel saw an advertisement praising the wonder of a night signalling lamp for Boy Scouts. Its light was said to be visible for half a mile, and it cost two-and-sixpence. The advertisement said no boy should be without one, and Dudley agreed !

" I'm going to send a postal order for one," Noel declared, producing his purse, and anxiously checking his small change.

"I'll buy one too," Malcolm said, carelessly producing two half-crowns, just as though he had no money problems to worry about. "In fact, I'll buy both and give them to you as a souvenir, Noel."

"I mustn't let you do that," protested Noel, much impressed by his chum's wealth. "It's a lot of money."

"Oh, tom-thumb to you," laughed Malcolm. "We'll get the postal order first thing after brekker. And catch the early post. Then for a quiet day!"

The breakfast gong vibrated from the hall. Mrs. Spraggart did not appear. She was in her bedroom, removing paper curlers and sipping tea, fussing and fuming as usual, therefore enjoying herself, and hoping her "chicks" would not get up to mischief during her absence.

Mr. Strathmore had a lot of things he wanted bought; tobacco, three reams of typing paper, and ink. Mrs. Strathmore reminded him of several things he had forgotten to pack for the holidays, including tooth paste, bathing costume and a new ribbon for his typewriter.

And slippers, too, for he had only packed one!

Then the children were asked whether they wanted anything "special", which meant each writing a list that Mrs. Spraggart would duly consider and cut down by half, for that good old soul ruled the Strathmores, children and parents alike, but very pleasantly. It was commonly thought that she spent all her wages in buying presents for each individual birthday, and for everyone at Christmas.

Even at home near London she could never visit the shops without bringing home a souvenir of her visit, for one or other, or all three of the children.

At nine o'clock the car was brought round to the front door, and those of the household not going assembled on the steps to yell " Good-bye " and wave, just as though the voyagers were off to America, by the way of Timbuctoo !

Two maids, the gardener and houseboy—not to mention James the cat (that Mrs. Spraggart would not allow out after nine o'clock at night) and Rover the sheep dog (that Mrs. Spraggart would not allow in the house after nine o'clock at night), stood in the background.

All were conscious that something " special " would be brought home. They had all given Mrs. Spraggart a list of things they wanted, Gwen and Dudley having solved such a problem on behalf of James the cat, and Rover·

Mrs. Spraggart arrived late on the scene, in a flowery dress that looked much too small, and a hat that was not only too large, but appeared to carry more flowers than Mr. Strathmore grew in his garden all the year round.

There were last-minute instructions to the maid, a reminder that Mr. Strathmore preferred his potatoes with jackets on, and James's fish for lunch was on the top of the cupboard in the cellar, and Rover was not to lick the dinner plates.

Then they were off, amid much shouting and waving.

" There, now," exclaimed Mr. Strathmore, quite

crossly, when the car had disappeared, " I haven't any large envelopes in the house, and they're not to be bought in this one-eyed place ! "

Mr. Strathmore always did forget the most important thing he wanted, though large envelopes had been his one lament for days, but Mrs. Spraggart would be sure to remember.

" Let's get my postal order off," proposed Malcolm to Noel. " And then for a lounge in the shadows somewhere."

" Your postal order ! I like that. Ours, you mean. I'm not letting you spend all your holiday money on me," protested Noel.

" You'll do as you're told or get your head punched," laughed Malcolm.

" Jolly decent of you ! "

" Don't be an ass," grandly from Malcolm. " What are you going to do today, Dud ? "

" Nothing much. Read, I expect."

Dudley knew very well what he intended to do. He wanted to go alone to the east cliff in the hope of seeing Bertet Carlsen. He was afraid that his new friend had been offended by Malcolm's conduct in the cave-mouth, and wanted to make sure Bertet didn't think Malcolm in the least mean, but strong-headed and a good sport.

Indeed, it was his intention to repeat Malcolm's apology in the boat on their return the same afternoon, and then all would be good friends again.

The two elder boys set off for the village.

The post office was really a cottage, with a few bottles of sweets in its small window, and a blue tin plate outside that squeaked when the wind blew, and on it was inscribed in white letters :

YOU MAY TELEPHONE FROM HERE

There were two steps down into the gloomy shop. Here one could buy stamps, sweets, tobacco, packets of stationery, paraffin, groceries, socks, stockings, papers and vegetables. It was Syre's emporium. Everything was muddled up with everything else. It was the happy playground of flies and, in due season, legions of wasps crawled there, or buzzed like explorers who had lost their way, and had no idea how to get home.

On a hot day, the cheap haberdashery smelt as strong as the waxy-looking cheese, with paraffin coming second, Faintly, in the background of such mingled odours, warm soap suds lingered like ghosts of yesteryear.

Old Mrs. Rattle—who kept the post office and general shop—was always washing, except when the bell clanged that called her from the tub into the shop. She did not take in other people's washing, but to be elbow-deep in foaming suds seemed her idea of taking life easily and very pleasantly.

Noel warned Malcolm about the two steps before he pushed the door open. The bell clanged. Coming from the strong sunlight into cavern-like gloom, he could see nothing for a few moments, but smelt everything Mrs. Rattle offered for sale at one sniff.

There was not much room in the shop, but he was surprised to collide with someone.

"Ah, my smuggler friends," said Mr. Spanyard, jovially.

Mr. Spanyard departed after that friendly remark. Noel was thankful that the gloom hid his flaming cheeks, for the presence of their friend reminded him of their quarrel.

Malcolm, however, was equal to the occasion, and remained haughty until the shop door closed behind Mr. Spanyard.

Mrs. Rattle was visible behind a small wire grill. That section of the shop she proudly called "The Post Office". She squinted curiously at a telegram form that Mr. Spanyard had handed to her. Whatever the condition of the weather, she never lighted the swing oil lamp until evening, in consequence of which she had become used to squinting at customers, at their money, at the goods she sold, and even at her washing, and now her face had become an everlasting squint, and was as wrinkled as a shrivelled apple.

"I would like a postal order for five shillings, and a tupenny-ha'penny stamp, please," said Noel, very politely.

He had waited some minutes, completely ignored, and thought that perhaps she was not conscious of their presence. She must have heard him, but continued to squint at the telegram form in her hand.

"You can wait, young man. The post office comes first," she told him sternly, in a voice that wheezed.

"Sorry."

The squinting lasted about another three minutes, and then she went to the telephone in a corner, having first to remove some tinned fruit stacked in front of the instrument.

"That the General?" she asked, in a thin, wavering voice, knowing the line only connected with the nearest General Post Office. "Syre Post Office speaking."

She shouted her loudest, which was not really loud. But her voice carried, and it carried across the street. The contents of telegrams sent from Syre Post Office were known to the inhabitants by virtue of the old dame's carrying voice. To send a telegram was her pride, and seldom was she gratified.

Whenever Mrs. Rattle had to declare her lawful occupation, she always wrote in a neat round hand, or said in her thin voice : "*On His Majesty's Service*," as if she was an envelope from Somerset House or Whitehall.

"Is that the General, miss? Mrs. Rattle, O.H.M.S. Syre, speaking. Take down telegram handed in at 9.41 this morning . . . Yes, this morning. Today! 'C for Christmas, e for England, r-r-r-r-r-r for r-r-radish. . . .' What's that? You can hear me! Then take down what I say. '*Certain tomorrow only night can attempt see to Jimmy kidnap and meet you early at sunset*'."

"That's from Mr. Spanyard," whispered Malcolm, breathlessly. "It may be a secret message."

"Anyway, why does he want to send a telegram?" asked Noel, interested. "Something about tomorrow night."

Malcolm tore off a telegram form from a bundle hanging from the wire grill. Mrs. Rattle did not see him or she would have had something to say about misusing "O.H.M.S. stationery".

However, she was informing the person at the other end of the line that it was "a lovely day for drying". Mrs. Rattle had two seasons in her year, it was either a lovely day for drying, or it was not!

The conversation continued on a personal note and at some length, and ended after Mrs. Rattle had given advice as to the best method of washing a bed quilt.

"Now, young man, don't keep me waiting. I've a tub full of curtains what's getting cold!"

She spoke crossly, and spent some minutes looking for the postal orders, which were eventually found under some pats of butter.

She scratched aside sundry oddments in a drawer, and then remembered that she had hidden the stamp book under a stack of firewood the previous night, a precaution known to everyone in the village.

Her dread was that "O.H.M.S. Property" might be stolen, and hid such property in all kinds of places when the shop was closed. She often forgot where to find things, but most of her customers could always remind her that the stamps were under the wood, the stamped postcards behind the biscuit tins, and money orders either beneath the butter or inside one of the tea caddies.

Having found the stamps, she remembered that the telegram had to be stamped. After that, she gave the wrong change, and Noel politely handed back an extra halfpenny.

" Lovely day for drying," she remarked, squinting at the returned coin.

" The kind of day Mrs. Spraggart likes for drying," answered Noel, only wishing to be polite.

" I don't know Mrs. Spraggart's opinions, but I know when it's a lovely day for drying," Mrs. Rattle answered quite sharply, and departed to her soap suds and curtains.

Outside in the road, Malcolm read the message he had written, word for word as Mrs. Rattle had communicated it over the phone.

" There is more in this message than meets the eye," was his verdict, but then Malcolm saw adventure in all kinds of unlikely happenings, and possessed a mind so imaginative that one could never have a dull minute with him, even during lazy moments after a swim.

Noel detected such gravity in his chum's voice that he really felt that the message was in code and, therefore, very, very mysterious.

" Doesn't it strike you as being queer, Noel, that Mr. Spanyard discouraged us from night smuggling last night, and tomorrow night—our great night, too—someone is to attempt to see Jimmy Kidnap. Whatever is likely to happen will happen then, which is why he wants us out of the way."

" But it's to happen at sunset, Malcolm. We're going to wait until it is dark."

" I know that, fathead. I believe it's a code message. Wish I had heard to whom it was sent. Do you remember ? "

" I know it was a telephone number, but I can't remember it," answered Noel.

" In that case, why didn't he telephone the message himself ? " asked Malcolm, frowning.

" I don't know," answered Noel, reasonably enough. "Perhaps because the only telephone in Syre is in the post office and Mrs. Rattle would hear if he was indiscreet. The message reads a bit funny to me."

" Funny ! " exclaimed Malcolm. " It's a code message, and I'm going to get to the bottom of it."

They strolled along the beach a little way, and then sat down. Malcolm puzzled his head over the message, trying to find an inner meaning.

Noel sprawled in the sun, and called his chum " an adventure-seeking fathead ! ", too warm and content to bother his brain about anything at the moment.

Eventually, Malcolm grew tired of his self-imposed task, though he remained stubborn that the message was in code.

After a long swim and a frolic in the sea, they sun-bathed for an hour, then it was time to return to lunch. The house seemed very strange and quiet without Mrs. Spraggart fussing around.

Dudley was a few minutes late for the meal, and seemed to be excited. He kept on flashing mystifying glances across the table at his brother and Malcolm.

Mr. Strathmore spoke once during the meal, rather crosly, to the effect that he had meant to ask Mrs. Spraggart to buy him some large envelopes and another pair of slippers, as one was useless to a two-legged man. It was quite possible the dear old soul would have both items on her list, and would buy a pair of slippers as gay as a flower-garden.

The voyagers were expected back for tea, so Mr. Strathmore reminded the boys to make themselves presentable by five o'clock. Within another week he hoped to finish the first draft of his book, and then he intended to go fishing, boating and swimming with the children.

Much to Dudley's annoyance and impatience, after lunch, Mr. Strathmore talked for a long time about future plans.

Finally, Mr. Strathmore remarked he really must get back to his writing, or the afternoon would be gone.

" What do you boys intend doing ? " he asked.

" Going for a short sail if the breeze holds, Dad," answered Noel. " She sails beautifully really."

" We haven't had a wind worth naming yet," complained Dudley. " I vote we have a swim. I don't want to row for miles and miles in this heat."

Out in the garden, Dudley breathlessly whispered : " I say, I saw Bertet Carlsen this morning."

" You needn't stick to that chap like glue," suggested Noel. " Better keep away from *the house*."

" Can't see why I should, anyway. You were thick enough with Bertet the last time you met him," Dudley protested, rather hotly. " I only saw him for a few moments. He told me *the house* was being watched ! "

" Who by ? " demanded Malcolm, eagerly.

" Bertet was using field-glasses from one of the upper windows," Dudley explained. " He saw a man on the cliff, and he was watching *the house* through field-glasses. That was early this morning."

" So that's what you're excited about. Did Bertet say anything about tomorrow night ? " asked Noel.

" He's leading the Preventive men," Dudley answered. " He's looking forward to the fun tremendously."

" You might as well know there is something queer going on, Dud," declared Malcolm, gravely. " There may be danger lurking around."

" Oh, don't rot, Malcolm. You like talking like that," laughed Noel, uneasy inwardly. " Let's do something. Let's stroll along to the cave. It wouldn't be fun to explore it without Gwen. That can wait until Dad takes a holiday."

The three set out, thoughtful and silent. It was

pleasant in the shade of the cave, with the muted tumble of the tide the only sound that hot, still afternoon.

A few gulls cruised lazily overhead, and a liner passed smokily through the haze along the horizon.

It was a sleepy afternoon and, except for another swim, the three boys were content to idle. No reference was made to the telegram, but Malcolm thought about it a great deal.

Against the sky, the House of Golden Windows stood out sharply. But they could not see it. It was coming into their lives, its history, and its secrets were soon to be an open book before them. It was, as it were, a loadstone rock that was drawing them relentlessly—others too— into an adventure even more thrilling and perilous than Malcolm Brewster had ever imagined.

CHAPTER XIII

THE SECRET MESSAGE

Mrs. Spraggart's arrival home, from her shopping expedition, was almost as exciting as her departure early that morning. She was invisible from the waist upwards, for she was heaped with parcels, which she would allow no one else to carry from the car to the house, so that only her skirt and shoes were visible.

Gwen rushed within doors with her purchases, and hid them before Dudley had a chance of guessing what the queer shapes could really be.

Mrs. Spraggart was quite surprised that the boys looked neat and clean, as good as gold, and suspected that torn garments and dirty towels were hidden somewhere.

And she simply daren't think what the bathroom looked like.

She asked most concernedly whether her " chick " had been " looked after ", and Dudley grinned sheepishly. James the cat miaowed as though starved, and immediately gained its point by receiving a second dinner and much petting.

Everyone seemed delighted to be together again.

Mrs. Spraggart regarded the journey as a daring adventure, just as though footpads and highwaymen were the order of the day, and that by her shrewd cunning she had brought Mrs. Strathmore and Gwen home safe in limb, mind and possessions.

" It's your chance, Dudley, while she's all sky-high," whispered Noel, meaning that now was the time to ask favours of old Mrs. Spraggart.

The chance was too good to be lost, so Dudley went in search of Mrs. Spraggart, who was in the kitchen telling the maid that she " never thought " to get back alive. Why or how she was there, to relate that simple journey, was a great mystery to her, but to no one else.

" And what does my chick want ? Drat the child, as if I have a single moment to spare."

Somewhat coy, reddening to the roots of his hair, Dudley opened his mouth several times, but somehow the words would not come out.

" Drat the chick, behaving like a gold fish out of water. Do say something ! "

She knew very well, by the symptoms, that a favour was to be asked, and frowned discouragingly, while in the depth of her generous heart it was already granted.

" Mrs. Spraggart, can I ask you something ? " pleaded Dudley, gravely, fumbling with a button.

" Of course not, you stupid child. I haven't a single moment to spare. Scarcely time for breathing. Run along, do ! You know very well I will not have you in the kitchen."

Dudley understood her symptoms as well as she understood his, and felt somewhat braver, for her crossness was a good omen.

" Please, Mrs. Spraggart, I want to ask a birthday favour of you."

" Birthday favour indeed ! Whose birthday may I be so bold as to ask ? I only know young gentlemen who are much too old and naughty to have birthdays, much less ask for favours."

" My birthday. It's tomorrow."

Mrs. Spraggart gasped, and her bushy eyebrows rose in surprise : " There now, if I had only known before ! But you wait until I get back from such a journey as never before, then tell me it's your birthday tomorrow. Well, all I can say is that you'll have to make do with a bright new shilling."

" I'd . . . I'd make do with your good wishes, Mrs. Spraggart, when tomorrow comes, thank you," answered Dudley, eagerly. " And a favour, if you don't mind in the least. I'd rather have the favour than the bright new shilling, if that would suit you just as well."

" Drat the chick ! Why don't you say what you want and not keep on hinting at a body ? Have you torn your knickers again and want me to forgive you ? "

" Oh, no, Mrs. Spraggart. But may I stop up really late tomorrow evening and play smugglers when it's dark ? Just as a big birthday favour, please ! "

Mrs. Spraggart thereupon gave a scream : " Of all things. Well, I never, never did ! "

" Just as a treat, Mrs. Spraggart," begged Dudley.

" Dear me, drat the child ! Aren't you bad enough already without wanting to be a smuggler ? And when it is dark of all nonsense."

" But you can only really be a smuggler when it is dark, Mrs. Spraggart."

The good old soul " hummed and hahed ", fidgeted and frowned, while all the time she knew she would agree. It was a birthday favour, otherwise her " chick " would have been " sent packing out of her kitchen with a flea in his ear ".

" And what do you think your dad and ma will say ? A smuggler of all things. They come to a bad end. All evil men do."

" Dad and Mum won't mind in the least if you don't, Mrs. Spraggart. I'm going to ask them when you say ' yes '."

" Of course I won't say ' yes '," she fussed, adding a

loud and rather prolonged sniff. "What time do you propose going to bed, if it is not an impudent question to ask a young gentleman?"

"Not really late, Mrs. Spraggart. It's dark enough by half-past nine."

"One hour later than usual then, as a birthday favour, Master Dudley," she promised, very grudgingly. "Dear me, how you children do talk a body round so. I don't know if I'm on my head or my heels." Then she suddenly smiled and her mild blue eyes twinkled: "My precious chick is eleven tomorrow. Too old to listen to stupid Mrs. Spraggart."

"Oh, no, never too old, Mrs. Spraggart. And thank you ever so much. I'll give you some contraband when it's safely run."

"Gracious me, do listen to the chick!" Mrs. Spraggart appeared to be frightened out of her very wits. "And don't you dare bring any evil contraband into this honest house. Really, but it's no good me saying anything. I am ruled by you children. Very well, one hour later than usual, Master Dudley, and not a moment later. Worrying me now, after what I have been through today. Run along with you, do!"

"Oh, thank you . . ."

"Run along, do!"

Mrs. Spraggart shooed her "chick" from the kitchen, and, within three minutes, Dudley had obtained permission of his parents who said, as usual: "You must ask

Mrs. Spraggart, and be careful you don't upset her first."

In a state of breathless excitement, the others were waiting in Noel's bedroom, almost as afraid as Dudley had been that Mrs. Spraggart would spoil everything.

They gave a great cheer when the " good news came through ", which brought Mrs. Spraggart pounding up the stairs, suspecting that some mischief was afoot.

" Do hurry and get ready for supper," she ordered, no less delighted by their joy than they themselves. " Master Noel, look at your hands ! "

" I've just washed, Mrs. Spraggart."

The children had taken great care to look clean and neat, with hair well brushed, and looking as innocent as lambs.

" And I would like to know what state the towels are in," she complained, as was her habit but not her nature. " Now, do behave yourselves for once," she shouted back, as she pounded down the stairs to the kitchen. " I've never had such a day ! "

They knew that Mrs. Spraggart was never happier than when she fussed and fumed, and kept on saying : " Drat ! ". She had a good reason for being in such a hurry-scurry, for there was the birthday cake to be iced, and a mysterious parcel to be wrapped up in pretty paper.

Gwen was eager to show Noel and Malcolm what she had bought for Dudley, and Noel wanted to test the clockwork speed-boat which his sister had purchased on his behalf, as a present for his young brother. One thin and another, Dudley seemed to be shooed away from everyone and out of every room, so he wandered in the garden.

During supper, Mrs. Spraggart said that they had better go to bed earlier than usual, which meant that Dudley had only half an hour to spare before being sent upstairs.

Gwen wanted to hear all over again plans for the night smuggling, and whether Dudley had seen Bertet, if so what were his plans, for it was known the smugglers were to make for the cave.

Malcolm continued to worry about the mysterious message, though he did not refer to it while one or both the younger children was near.

Gwen and Noel went for a short stroll down the drive, while Noel and Malcolm climbed and squatted on a branch of a tree at the edge of the cliff, from where they could obtain a bird's eye view of the village and harbour, above which rose the east cliff and *the house*, the windows of which were already pale gold.

It was a very lovely evening. The tide rippled lazily over the sands, and broke soundlessly amid the boulders. No huge waves broke to foam and hiss, throwing up spray, but melted into the parent body or lapped amid the boulders as though too tired for effort.

Gwen was anxious to hear all about the plans for the following night, and whether Bertet had agreed to lead the Preventive men.

" Oh, yes, Gwen, if he possibly can. But he must be careful. I am to leave my bedroom light on before we set out," Dudley explained. " He can see it easily, and will know we have set out for the cliffs. Bertet has a tent in his garden and is allowed to sleep there, but he is guarded. It may not be possible for him to come."

" Guarded ! " Gwen's eyes grew large with surprise.

" He didn't say why he is guarded, Gwen. He doesn't say much about himself. The guard sleeps in another tent nearby, and won't turn in until eleven o'clock. Bertet must be back by then."

" I feel awfully excited about it all, Dudley, just as though something really exciting is going to happen," whispered Gwen. " Suppose Bertet can't come, that will spoil the fun."

" Then you must lead the Preventive men, Gwen. If Bertet isn't waiting for us by the door in the wall, we shall know he can't come."

" Oh, you must be leader if Bertet isn't there," protested Gwen. " Who has ever heard of a girl leading Preventive men ? "

Dudley had always been a follower and felt himself to be incapable of taking Bertet's place, if the need were to arise. He was about to argue the point when he saw a dusky figure approach beneath the overhanging trees, at the entrance to the drive.

" Ah, my young friends, this will save me from calling. I have brought your photographs."

It was Count Aland, looking very smart in a brass-buttoned blue coat, white shoes, and flannels, and a peak cap with a white top and gold crest.

" My father and mother will be very pleased to see you, sir," suggested Gwen, for she never forgot her manners as Dudley did now and again.

Dudley was eagerly glancing at the photographs the Count had handed to him.

" Oh, Gwen, this is a spiffing one of us all ! "

" I will not call now, thank you," smiled Count Aland, addressing himself to Gwen. " I haven't a moment to spare, but I realised you would be anxious about your photographs. They are very good."

Count Aland seemed to be as pleased with the prints as they were, and asked who their young friend was, the boy with so many weapons in his sash, who looked so handsome and brave.

" He lives in *the house* on the east cliff," answered Gwen, readily. " Oh, do look at this one ! Fierce Fred looks sulky. Ha, ha, but Noel looks so tall and grand."

" And who is Fierce Fred ? " inquired the Count.

" My brother's school friend, Malcolm Brewster, sir," answered Dudley. " I say, what a lovely ship," he exclaimed, turning to the last print. " Noel didn't say he went out to her."

" You and your sister must come aboard my yacht very soon," invited the Count. " I will call and ask your parents to join me in a short cruise. And perhaps your young friend from *the house* would like to join us."

" I wish he could," regretted Dudley. " But he isn't really allowed to leave the garden."

" Well, well, I must see what can be done about that," promised the Count. " I will do some more prints and let you have them. Good-night. I am really sorry I cannot call upon your parents now."

He patted Dudley in a friendly manner on the shoulder, and gave Gwen a tin of toffees before he passed into the heavy shadows amid the trees.

Gwen and Dudley ran off to find the elder boys, and to show them the photographs.

Malcolm, as soon as he had looked at the prints, argued that he did not look sulky in one of them, but fierce and ruthless as a " Devon Smuggler " should look.

Mrs. Spraggart thought the photographs were " lovely ", and then bundled Dudley off to bed.

An hour later, the two elder boys followed, but not to fall asleep. Malcolm was still worrying about the mysterious message sent by Mr. Spanyard that morning. In the dim light of their bedroom, he examined it again.

" Oh, pack it up, man," impatiently from Noel, who never wanted to hear another word about the message again. " You simply love to make mountains out of molehills, Malcolm. That photo of me standing by the boulder, waving my sword . . ."

" Noel, I've got it ! " cried Malcolm, leaping out of bed and leaping upon Noel's. " Listen ; *' Certain to-*

morrow only night can attempt see to Jimmy kidnap and meet you early at sunset'. It's the word 'kidnap' and 'early at sunset' which made me think. Ask yourself, Noel, sunset can't really be late or early, but only sunset. And 'kidnap' is a funny name, don't you think?"

"Perhaps you're right, Malcolm," answered Noel, without interest. "But I can't see what you're so excited about, and if you shout again and jump on my bed, Mrs. Spraggart will come up and make a scene."

"Read only the second and then every other word!" whispered Malcolm, thrusting the message into his chum's hand, triumphant and excited.

Noel read aloud as he was directed: "'*Tomorrow night attempt kidnap meet early sunset*'."

They stared into each other's eyes.

"Kidnap who?" asked Noel, wide-eyed.

"We can only guess, Noel. It can't be any of the local people. That leaves us, the Count and Bertet Carlsen!"

"No wonder Mr. Spanyard didn't want us playing smugglers and spoiling his game," whispered Noel, breathlessly. "We . . . we must do something!"

"Of course we must! No one would be kidnapped in daylight, Noel. Not in a place like this. We must first find out who Mr. Spanyard is meeting at sunset and where. Then, when we really know who is to be kidnapped, we must warn them."

"But where is Mr. Spanyard meeting someone?" asked Noel.

" He's meeting his gang, of course, Noel ! They are to meet at sunset and ' early ' means Earlie Cove. I'm sure it does."

A breathless silence followed.

" Hadn't we better tell Dad ? "

" Not until we really know what we are talking about," suggested Malcolm. " You and I must hide at Earlie Cove and listen. That will give us time to get back and tell your father what we find out. It won't be dark, but the kidnappers will wait until it's dark, and we shall know by then who they are to kidnap and where."

" I believe they're after Bertet."

" So do I," agreed Malcolm, gravely. " Dudley said tonight that he is guarded. I say, I've got a spiffing plan. The kidnappers will never suspect us of knowing about them. Gwen and Dudley are to meet Bertet. They must bring him back to the house for safety."

" No one would think of looking in our house for him," agreed Noel. " And then we could tell Dad, and fetch the police."

" Of course. But half a mo'," warned Malcolm. " It won't do to tell those two kids anything until we're sure. They'll become so excited that Mrs. Spraggart will suspect, and you know Dud tells her everything."

" You're right there," answered Noel, readily. " But how are we going to get rid of the kids tomorrow evening, early ? We shall have to get to Earlie Cove soon after tea, and hide."

" Oh, well, we shall have to dodge them somehow. Look here, after tea I'll propose hide-and-seek. You and I to be the first to hide. Then, as soon as we get back from Earlie Cove, we must tell the kids everything. If it's Bertet the gang is after, Gwen and Dudley must meet him and bring him back to the house. If they go inland and keep to the woods, they won't be seen."

" It's a bit risky," said Noel, thoughtfully. " Hadn't you better meet Bertet ? "

" We've got to be frightfully cunning, Noel. You and I will have to set out in the boat as though we're going to play night smugglers. Mr. Spanyard will see us, and wait until we return before he acts. That will give Gwen and Dudley heaps of time."

" You're right there, Malcolm. But wouldn't it be better to tell Dad ? "

" Later, you ass ! Can't you see that if we act too quickly and the police come, Mr. Spanyard will lie doggo, and we shan't be able to prove a thing against him ? Besides, he may not be after Bertet. There is the Count ! I vote we find out all we can first."

Noel had allowed his chum to lead too often in the past to offer resistance now, apart from the fact that Malcolm seemed so sure of himself that Noel had every confidence in him.

" After all, your pater may not believe us," warned Malcolm. " Grown-ups think chaps our age know nothing. Better find out all we can first. And don't tell the kids until the very last minute."

It was late before they fell asleep that night. They had been to Earlie Cove once, and knew that there were plenty of hiding places. Malcolm's scheme seemed so easy, and the right one, that Noel agreed to everything he suggested, both taking a solemn oath to keep their secret until they were sure what Mr. Spanyard's game was, and they had discovered the victim of his vile plotting.

CHAPTER XIV

DANGER

DUDLEY awoke early the next morning, as any right-minded boy should do on his birthday. It seemed that the house would never be active. He imagined all the presents he would get, which made time pass even more slowly.

At long last, Gwen came into his bedroom, and they played " Guessing the presents ". Gwen was delighted because he was wrong every time.

" Oh, roll on breakfast," shouted Dudley, jumping up

and down on his bed. " I do believe you're going to give me a smuggler's costume, Gwen."

" Wrong again ! " She clapped her hands in delight.

At last, they heard Mrs. Spraggart " fussing and fuming ".

Dudley dashed for the bathroom and, as soon as he was dressed, ran down the drive to wait for the postman. Back at the house, everyone was busy wrapping up mysterious presents, and in the excitement the two elder boys forgot how thrilling was to be the sunset hour that evening.

The postman brought several parcels, and a heap of birthday cards for Dudley, so it was no wonder he felt too excited to eat when the gong was sounded for breakfast.

Mrs. Spraggart gave her " chick " a hug that nearly crushed him. Her present was huge, but she made him open all his other parcels first, the family as eager as himself to find out what the contents were.

A cycle from his parents was a breathless discovery. He simply had to ride it just once round the breakfast-room, and Mrs. Spraggart became the first pedestrian casualty. But she laughed as she toppled and clung to the table, " dratting " her " chick " with what breath she had left in her body, pretending to be hurt, whereas the cycle had scarcely touched her skirt.

Noel's speed-boat was reserved for later experiments in the bath. Gwen gave him an electric lamp for the cycle, that could be dimmed. Malcolm produced an air-gun. Finally, Mrs. Spraggart's huge parcel received attention. It contained a wheel-barrow and garden tools, with several packets of seeds that should have been sown quite three months before.

Mrs. Spraggart became very stern, and made Dudley eat his breakfast, after which he was allowed to "try" the cycle again, with Gwen's lamp attached.

" I shan't be long," he shouted, as they watched him depart down the drive, Mrs. Spraggart shouting to him not to go too fast.

The children were to spend the morning as they wished, but during the afternoon the parents and Mrs. Spraggart were to join in their games, and after tea they were to " amuse " themselves.

Dudley felt himself to be a very important person on his birthday. Like old Mrs. Spraggart, he scarcely had time in which to breathe. He wanted to do a little gardening, for that would delight the good old soul, and play all kinds of games with the others.

It was not until after tea, when Mrs. Spraggart was redder and more breathless than ever before in her life, following a sail in the *Gallant*, and Mr. and Mrs. Strathmore felt that they had earned a quiet read, when Malcolm and Noel had a chance to get away to Earlie Cove, without hurting anyone's feelings.

However, before they went, a most important confab was held.

" Now listen, you kids." Malcolm addressed Gwen

and Dudley as though he was much older and had the right to rule their lives. They were both quite impressed. " We've got a secret to share, and you've got to promise to say nothing until I say you may."

Noel muttered : " It's frightfully serious ! "

Gwen and Dudley instantly became solemn, for never before had Noel seemed so grave. Both he and Malcolm had decided earlier that it would be mean to deceive " the kids " by pretending to play hide-and-seek.

Malcolm told them about the mysterious message sent by Mr. Spanyard, and that Noel and himself proposed to spy on Mr. Spanyard at Earlie Cove that very evening.

" Hadn't . . . hadn't we better tell Father ? " suggested Gwen, very round-eyed.

" That's just what a girl would say," remarked Malcolm, grandly. " But we must first make sure I'm right about the message. You two kids hang around until we get back."

Dudley, though he looked so frail and always turned to Gwen when he was troubled, surprised the others by saying : " I must warn Bertet. He's my chum and I'm going to stand by him, whatever happens."

" Bravo," from Malcolm. " But wait until we get back. I've got a spanking plan and it is sure to work. Mr. Spanyard won't make a move until it is dark, so we've plenty of time to spare."

The elder boys departed, heading for Earlie Cove via the cliff-top, and not along the beach.

Gwen and Dudley kept away from their parents so that inquiry should not be made after the two elder boys.

Fortunately, Mrs. Spraggart had suggested a " picnic supper ", which she had already packed as " contraband ". None was likely to take interest in them for some hours.

Dudley was not in the least afraid on his own behalf now that he worried about Bertet Carlsen. He and Gwen had a long, patient wait, and the hour dragged.

The only ray of comfort for Dudley was that he had arranged to meet Bertet when it was dusk, and that Mr. Spanyard was not likely to make a move until it was quite dark.

Gwen, fearing her small brother would work himself into a " state of nerves ", suggested perhaps it was not Bertet who was in danger of being kidnapped.

" But I feel Bertet is in danger, Gwen," insisted Dudley. " And only we can help him. By the time we have told Father—and he may not believe there is any real danger—and the police arrive, it may be much too late."

Meanwhile, keeping amid the bushes as much as possible, Noel and Malcolm hastened towards Earlie Cove, which was about one mile east along the coast, and a little more by way of the cliffs.

Earlie Cove was a very isolated spot that looked as though the cliff had fallen years ago. The approach to the cove was down a steep descent of broken ground, full of hollows and humps, that was thickly covered in bushes down to the water.

There was only a small stretch of sand suitable for landing, and it was here the two boys expected " the gang " to arrive.

" Lucky the bushes reach almost to the water's edge," whispered Malcolm, as they began to crawl through the undergrowth. " We shall be able to hear every word said on an evening so quiet."

It was an hour or more before sunset, and the waiting was a great trial. Malcolm began to feel that he was not so clever as he liked to be thought, yet he could not help thinking that he had made no mistake.

" We can easily get back without being spotted with all these bushes all over the place," whispered Noel, rather anxiously.

" Rather ! "

Imperceptibly, the light changed and, from an almost blinding brilliance off the sea, it turned into a glow. It would be some time before *the house* on the east cliff would have golden windows, but Malcolm declared : " It's sunset now, really. Any moment anything exciting may happen ! "

" Suppose they do not come ? "

" Oh, there's heaps of time yet," less heartily from Malcolm. He had not considered what he would do if he proved to be wrong, and the realisation that Mr. Spanyard might not come to Earlie Cove made him feel anxious. He made up his mind not to despair until the gloaming made the cliffs and sea indistinct.

Though time lagged for them, actually they had not much longer to wait before they heard the chug-chug of a motor-boat hidden beyond the narrow inlet of the cove.

Before the craft actually appeared, Mr. Spanyard arrived, having come via the beach. He was dressed in a blue jersey and serge trousers, and looked very stern. Malcolm thought that his hip pocket bulged, and his imaginative mind leapt to the conclusion that the man was armed.

The motor-boat glided into the cove. Four men leapt ashore, to gather round Mr. Spanyard on the sand. The party was not more than a yard or so from the hidden boys.

No order was given, but the craft turned and chugged out to sea.

The chums held their breath for an instant. Both thought the gang would make for *the house*, and they intended to follow, unless opportunity gave them a chance to escape before that.

As Noel had remarked, the bushes would allow them to get away without danger of being seen, though they would have to take great care crossing the height of the cliff farther along.

" You fellows know what is expected of you," said Mr. Spanyard, apparently in no hurry, for he had lighted his pipe and now sprawled on the sands at ease. " You've got to scatter amid the bushes opposite *the house*, and not act until the signal is given. We can't move until it's dusk, at the earliest. Don't want to be seen against the skyline from the yacht."

" You've had a busy time," one of the men remarked.

" When the Count came, I did a bit of spying. I have received information that tonight's the night. I'd better warn you chaps there are some lively youngsters who may be smuggling tonight. Don't let them see you, that's all."

Apparently, whatever the plan was those men were well versed in every detail, and their talk became casual and unimportant. But the two spying boys had heard enough to realise that " the gang " were interested in the House of Golden Windows.

Malcolm signalled to Noel, and they began to creep between the bushes, scarcely daring to move more than an inch at the time, until the height was reached.

" It's Bertet they're after," breathed Noel.

" Yes, or someone else in *the house* ! "

The house was sharply etched against the sky, its windows turning pale golden. The harbour seemed to be a long way off, but the Count's yacht was clearly visible in almost every detail. It was an evening of remarkable visibility, so that even cottages dotted here and there inland, and on the hills far away, were amazingly clear, and seemed to be very much nearer than usual.

They ran some of the way. There was no need to be cautious now that they were away from Earlie Cove.

They reached the drive, hot and breathless. The " two

kids " were anxiously waiting for them amid the trees by the gate.

" Now listen, you kids," whispered Malcolm, earnestly. " There isn't a minute to be lost. A pretty tough gang has landed at Earlie Cove, and later they're going to watch *the house*. They won't move until it is really dark. We've got to act. No time to warn anyone."

" I must warn Bertet, Malcolm . . ."

" I'm coming to that, Dudley. It won't be dusk for another half-hour, and Bertet won't leave the garden until then." Malcolm appeared very confident that they could handle the situation, and his self-assurance inspired the others. " You two kids must get off now and be careful you are not seen. Hide amid the bushes close to the door, and as soon as Bertet appears, tell him his life is in danger. Bring him back to this house. Don't come through the village, but keep to the woods inland. You know the way."

" Rather," muttered Dudley. Amazing, he was not afraid, but even eager. " I'll hide Bertet in my bedroom."

" Look here, it's not safe for you kids to risk going," declared Noel, anxiously. " Father will have to know. He and I could fetch Bertet . . ."

" You're right," admitted Malcolm. It's . . . it's too dangerous . . ."

" But we must take the risk," spoke up Gwen, white and determined. " Dad and Mum went for a car ride about half an hour ago, and I don't know when they will be home."

" Then we've got to do something," Noel told them. " But Malcolm and myself had better fetch Bertet . . ."

" I've thought of that, Noel," interrupted Malcolm. " I reckon the motor-boat is waiting, and if Gwen and Dudley fail to save Bertet, we two will have to do so. If they see the *Gallant* off shore, they won't risk signalling their boat."

" But we can't tackle men," protested Noel.

" I know we can't. But if we search and find a motor-boat, there may be only one man aboard her," argued Malcolm. " Our last hope is to prevent them from escaping by sea."

" It's no good talking here all night what we are going to do," impatiently from Dudley. " Malcolm is right. And none will attack Gwen and me, anyway. The *Gallant* may be mistaken for a coastguard boat, or something, and that may frighten them away."

" Not only that," exclaimed Noel, as a bright idea flashed across his mind. " There's Count Aland. We had better row out to him."

" Why didn't you think of that before ? " asked Gwen, somewhat relieved. " Oh, do let's hurry, Noel. Bertet may be kidnapped ! "

" There's plenty of time," assured Malcolm. " But you two might as well get ahead and wait for Bertet. Mr. Spanyard warned his gang we might be smuggling, so I don't think any harm will happen to you. And that lot won't move until it's dark."

Noel watched his brother and sister disappear into the shadows, with some misgiving tugging at his heart.

" Plucky kids, those two ! " admiringly from Noel.

" Rather ! I believe Dudley would die to save Bertet. And Gwen's a jolly good sticker," answered Malcolm. " But I wouldn't have sent them if I thought there was real danger. Pity your Dad isn't home, though."

" We're a couple of fatheads," admitted Noel, a moment later. " We ought not to have kept what we knew to ourselves."

Clearly, it was no good having regrets. Now that the quiet, dimming hour of twilight was upon them, both sharply realised for the first time how serious and even dangerous was the game they were playing.

" We must wait until it's dark before we go to the ship, or Mr. Spanyard may see and suspect," warned Malcolm. " If he sees us making for the yacht, instead of playing smugglers, he will wonder what we are up to. If Bertet's sharp on time, they will get away and home before Spanyard and his gang move from Earlie Cove."

So much depended on whether Mr. Spanyard waited until it was quite dark. The two boys were sure he would wait, for to keep a strange craft off shore at sunset would attract attention.

" We had better risk seeing the Count," advised Noel. " I don't expect Mr. Spanyard is down at the harbour. Let's go ! "

They set off for the harbour.

The House of Golden Windows looked grey and mysterious in the gloaming. It was fated to bring adventure and danger into their lives that night, and the story of its secret was about to be revealed to them.

But their excitement was such that neither realised that cunning men thwarted are sometimes merciless.

Neither did they remember that Mr. Spanyard had promised to help them, whenever they cared to ask for his aid !

CHAPTER XV

THE ATTACK

DUDLEY had seldom shown a great deal of courage in standing up for himself, but had always had Gwen or old Mrs. Spraggart to fight his battles for him, yet on that shadowy evening, when he and his sister set out to warn Bertet of danger, he was not afraid. With Gwen by his side, he felt conscious that it was his duty to protect her.

To reach the top of the east cliff, without passing through the village, they had to go rather a long way round. They held hands as they hastened, little knowing what every bush and almost every shadow might hide.

They arrived, breathless and tense, by the door in the

wall that surrounded *the house*, and crouched behind some nearby bushes.

Everything around them was fast becoming indistinct and unreal, even the massive wall. The brightness had faded from the sky that was now blue-black, and a lone star shone like the signal light of an unknown watcher.

It was so very quiet that they scarcely dared to breathe. They felt themselves to be in a strange world, quite alone, for even nature seemed to be holding its breath, as though waiting for something terrible to happen.

The waiting was long and rather frightening, with only their anxious thoughts to keep them company. Neither spoke, but they held hands, and felt all the braver for each other's company.

" Perhaps Bertet isn't coming tonight," whispered Dudley, eventually. " I switched on my bedroom light as a signal. It must be long past the time he promised to meet me."

" It isn't really late, Dud."

But Gwen felt, too, that it must be nearly midnight.

The door was almost invisible. They kept on glancing around, trying to peer through the heavy dusk.

There were men hidden amid the bushes on the cliff-top. Each man was watching and waiting, not knowing that two children nearby were alarmed and anxious about a friend who might appear at any moment.

The hidden men were too far away from the door to see it through the heavy gloom. That was fortunate, for none of them saw the door open, inch by inch, and a boy slip out.

"Bertet, we must run. Men are going to kidnap you!"

Dudley's tense, low voice did not carry, but it reached the keen ears of a man some yards away. He began to creep stealthily upon them.

"Oh, quick, Bertet," Gwen pleaded, as Bertet drew himself up proudly and stared defiantly into the gloom. "We must hide you."

For a few fated moments, Bertet hesitated, not fully understanding how earnest was Gwen, doubting and stubborn in his desire not to show fear.

"Pleese, we play Preventive men."

The man, creeping upon them, was very close. He could not clearly catch their low, breathless whispering.

"We must hide you, Bertet. There is danger," Dudley again warned his friend.

"Pleese, but it dis a coward to run and hide," protested Bertet. "And surely I must for to warn my friends."

"You're not to risk returning now." Dudley caught Bertet by the arm. "And we're powerless against some men. We're going to hide you for a little while."

Bertet hesitated.

The white faces of his friends, and their earnest appeal not to ask questions until later, convinced him there was not a minute to be lost.

As they turned to run between the bushes in the direction of the wood, on the farther side of the wall there came the sound of crashing undergrowth.

Startled, they raced away from the sounds, and crouched behind some bushes, fearing their retreat was cut off. Dimly, they watched two men struggle desperately. One was Mr. Spanyard, but they did not recognise him.

It was a brief struggle, and then all was quiet, except for someone breathing very deeply.

Mr. Spanyard's jersey was torn off his back, and his powerful chest was quivering after such exertion that he felt weak. There was an unconscious man at his feet, a giant of a fellow, who was dressed in a sailor's bell-bottomed trousers and a dark shirt, through the torn sleeve of which his arm was white and slippery with sweat.

Mr. Spanyard had not remained long at Earlie Cove, after Noel and Malcolm had departed earlier that evening. He had returned to Syre, by way of the beach, where he had waited in the doorway of his cottage, using binoculars on the yacht in the harbour.

Later, he had passed rapidly along the cobbled street, making for the top of the east cliff.

Having gained the height, he had crawled amid the bushes until he chanced upon a man lying and watching *the house*. Mr. Spanyard had heard Dudley and Bertet whispering. As the man had crept upon the three children, so Mr. Spanyard had closed in upon him, and then had sprung and borne the stranger to the ground.

Now, panting and tearing off his torn jersey, Mr. Spanyard stared around. But the children had disappeared. An anxious frown furrowed his forehead.

Next, he gave a low whistle that could easily have been mistaken for the cry of a night bird.

A man appeared in response to the signal.

The unconscious man opened his eyes, and bared his teeth in a snarl. Mr. Spanyard's companion knelt and, seizing the man's arms, quickly lashed his wrists together with a piece of torn shirt he had wrenched off the victim's body.

" Gag him, Harris," ordered Mr. Spanyard, removing the victim's belt and securing his ankles with it.

Harris used a piece of shirt as a gag. The prisoner struggled feebly, for he was still under the drugging effect of the punch to jaw, which Mr. Spanyard had so ably given.

There were other men amid the scattered bushes. Some had heard but had not seen that brief, fierce struggle of two powerful, desperate men.

None stirred, however, for they were well-disciplined, and waited for a signal.

" He's a sailor," whispered Harris, stooping low over the bound man.

" A foreigner off the yacht," said Mr. Spanyard, in a low voice. " Three of my young friends are playing smugglers hereabouts. Your job is to find them and take them home. It is dangerous to be on the cliff tonight."

" Leaving this fellow here ? " asked Harris.

" Yes, for the time being. I don't think the fight has attracted attention, or the whole scheme might have been ruined," whispered Mr. Spanyard. " Six men set out from the yacht, and landed at the foot of the cliff. There are five left now, somewhere close to us."

" I shall never find those children without falling into trouble myself," said Harris. " Are the others making for this door in the wall ? "

" Those men from the yacht will make for the door," said Mr. Spanyard, in a voice so low that it would not have been heard three yards away. " All you have to do is to find three children and get them out of harm's way. Search the bushes close to the wall."

Harris disappeared towards the wall. Mr. Spanyard, having made sure the prisoner's bonds were secure, rolled him beneath some bushes, and crouched himself.

Fortunately, Bertet and his two young friends had not run towards the road that led to the iron entrance gates of *the house*. They did not know it then, but their retreat was cut off. They had taken the opposite direction by mistake.

" Pleese, for what should we do now ? " asked Bertet, for they suddenly realised their mistake. " There will be much trub-bel for you and I am sorry for it."

" Oh, but it's not your fault," whispered Gwen, who realised she must not allow herself to be afraid and lose

G

her head. "It's that horrid Mr. Spanyard, and he seemed to be so nice. What do you think we ought to do, Dud?"

Dudley had never before been appealed to, and the surprising fact that Gwen, of all people, was looking to him to make a decision, helped a great deal to strengthen his nerves.

"For one thing," he answered in a voice not quite so steady as he wished, "we've run in the wrong direction, and now we can't reach either the wood or our house."

"Pleese, why?"

"There are men on the cliff, Bertet."

"But we hide in my garden, no?"

"I'm afraid there are men close to the door," answered Dudley. "I'm not at all sure what is happening, except you are in danger, and the sooner we're away from *the house*, the better."

Bertet looked grave.

"You see," exclaimed Dudley, "Mr. Spanyard thinks we're playing at smugglers, and if I were caught it wouldn't matter much. He would not harm me. But you must hide, while I go for help."

"Oh, Dudley!" admiringly from Gwen.

"Mr. Spanyard wouldn't want to kidnap me, Gwen. I must get down to the beach and try to attract Noel's attention. Then, when they come in-shore, I will fetch you two and we can all escape in the *Gallant*."

"Pleese, that dis ver' good, but if you shout . . ."

" I'm not shouting for the boat. We've got to be jolly cautious," warned Dudley, gravely. " I shall signal with my torch. Noel taught me a little Morse. But, if I'm not back within half an hour, try to reach the wood and hide there until day."

Gwen was no less equal to the occasion : " We shall be all right, Dud, and if you're not back within half an hour, we'll hide in the wood."

" Pleese, you are in trub-bel with me," Bertet whispered, very concerned for their welfare, and not in the least anxious about himself. " You must go home. It dis safer you without me. Ja ! "

" Mr. Spanyard doesn't want us, and we're in no real danger," declared Dudley. " But we're not going to leave you. If I only find Noel and he comes in with the boat, escape would be easy."

Gwen thought so, too.

" You two remain here for about half an hour. And, Gwen, you won't be frightened ? " asked Dudley.

" I'll try ever so hard not to be." She choked down her tears.

" And I will surely look after your sister," promised Bertet, bravely. " I will see her safe for you. I will allow no one for to touch your sister."

Dudley hesitated a moment.

Now that it came to going off alone, across that quiet, dark cliff, he faltered. He suddenly kissed Gwen, and vanished.

It was the silence that was so terrible. Waiting behind a bush, thinking something might happen any moment, made one's nerves taut.

Gwen thought : " I mustn't be a silly little goose," and forced down her tears.

Dudley threaded his way amid the bushes, listening at every step. He kept well away from those bushes in line with the door in the wall, and felt relief when he reached the edge of the cliff.

He crawled along until he came to where the cliff had broken away long ago, leaving an easy way down to the beach.

Reaching the shore, he hesitated behind a boulder, listening. A few yards away, the tide muttered as it tumbled, and now and again it was very still for a breathless moment, as though it, too, was afraid of what might be hidden in the darkness.

The nearby waters looked like a dull mirror, across the surface of which now and again long, slow-moving ripples approached the shore.

But the darkness was too deep for Dudley to see many yards. The *Gallant* would not carry lights, and he found that he had lost his torch while crawling among the bushes.

He wished now that the oars and rowlocks had not been muffled, for then he would have heard her off-shore. Dudley thought more about his sister and Bertet than he did of his own welfare.

The suspense tugged at his nerves.

Finally, he despaired of sighting the *Gallant* and, not daring to wait too long, Dudley hastened to rejoin his sister and friend. On gaining the cliff-top, he stood listening for some minutes. The silence somehow puzzled him.

A light here and there shone from the village. Soon the moon would break the darkness and the long, deep twilight of a summer night would make their position more perilous. Frightening though the heavy darkness was, it was more friendly than moonlight would have been that night.

Little then did he know how unfortunate it was that Mr. Spanyard had not recognised Bertet Carlsen when he came from the garden but, in the brief, vague glimpse he had caught of the children, had not recognised them.

Dudley felt very much the man on his eleventh birthday, and behaved like one. He did not consider himself. He was alarmed on behalf of his sister and Bertet Carlsen.

Furthermore, Dudley was sure that Mr. Spanyard would not harm Gwen or himself.

Only Bertet was in real danger !

Men become brave—though they feel afraid—when those they love need help and protection. Gwen and Bertet needed his help that night !

He approached where they were hidden, very stealthily.

CHAPTER XVI

THE CAPTIVE

MR. SPANYARD had left Earlie Cove shortly after Noel and Malcolm had set off across the cliff-top, to return along the beach to Syre.

For some time, Mr. Spanyard smoked, lounging against the harbour wall, apparently without a care or interest in the world.

When the twilight deepened and the shadows lengthened, he went into his cottage.

Later, he came to the doorway, and swept the east cliff with a pair of night-glasses and, now and again, he focused his attention on the yacht that looked rather ghostly in the fading light.

So preoccupied was Mr. Spanyard that he failed to see Noel and Malcolm pause just beyond the doorway. The boys were surprised to see the shadowy outline of the man, believing him to be with his comrades at Earlie Cove.

"Spying on the Count's yacht," whispered Malcolm, tugging his chum by the arm as a hint they should hasten down to the boat before Mr. Spanyard saw them.

At that moment, however, Mr. Spanyard lowered his glasses. He seemed neither surprised nor displeased to see them. He was most friendly.

"Ah, my smuggler friends !" he smiled. "But not dressed for the part ?"

"We're not playing smugglers," said Malcolm, coldly. "Changed our minds."

"I am glad you have not ignored my advice," Mr. Spanyard told them. "Tomorrow, I hope to be able to tell you why. Believe me, I only want to be your friend."

He trained his binoculars on the east cliff again, ignoring the two boys.

"We'll have to wait until it's darker before we go to the yacht," whispered Malcolm. "I hope he doesn't see the two kids and Bertet."

"The light's too poor to see them from here," answered Noel, in a subdued tone of voice. "Within half an hour it will be almost totally dark for about an hour."

Mr. Spanyard lowered his glasses.

"I suppose it must almost be your bedtime," he said, pleasantly. "I don't want to spoil your fun. I only want to warn you, it's best to keep away from the cliff tonight. Sorry, I can't say more for the moment."

"Oh, that's all right, Mr. Spanyard," answered Malcolm. "We're not going to the cliff."

"I see," he answered, surprised. "I suppose you have strolled down to have a look at your boat? Going to make her snug for the night, in true sailor fashion? Look here, I'm sorry about our little quarrel. Perhaps you'll think better of me tomorrow."

"Why tomorrow?" Malcolm was suspicious that the man was trying to draw them, and learn what their intention was that night.

Mr. Spanyard shrugged his shoulders, and again trained his night-glasses on the yacht.

"Much can happen during the night," he remarked, a moment later. "Tomorrow morning I may have an interesting story to tell you. You both must be curious to know why I am so mysterious, and why I am watching now."

"Well, suppose we are?" retorted Malcolm, embarrassed.

"Natural, you should be," smiled Mr. Spanyard. "Tomorrow you shall know everything. Trust me until then. How is your friend, the Count? Everything is very quiet and dark aboard his ship. Almost, don't you think, as though he doesn't want his movements watched ! Last night the yacht was a blaze of lights."

He became intent upon the east cliff.

Suddenly, his figure stiffened as though gripped by suspense. He had seen something that had startled him but he recovered his composure a second later.

The heavy dusk prevented the naked eyes from identifying anything clearly beyond a few yards.

The two boys waited, alarmed that he had seen Gwen and Dudley.

Mr. Spanyard hastened into his cottage, and returned a moment later without his binoculars. He seemed surprised to see the two boys in the street.

"Forgot you two chaps," he again smiled, but not naturally or pleasantly. "It's time you were both in bed, you know. I can't stop. I . . . I . . . have just remembered I promised to make a call."

He hastened up the cobbled street, as one in a great hurry. He was disturbed, even alarmed. The two boys stared after him, puzzled by his strange conduct.

"He's making for the cliff. He saw something there ! " muttered Noel, anxiously.

"Yes, and I hope it wasn't the kids he saw. It might have been a signal he's been waiting for," suggested Malcolm. "I wonder why he returned here ? And what's happened to his gang at Earlie Cove ? "

"I'm more curious about the yacht," answered Noel. "I think Mr. Spanyard wants to be our friend, and I think he is right about the yacht. It's queer she's in darkness and so quiet. Her bow is now towards the harbour-mouth."

"Never mind the yacht now! I don't like those two kids being on the cliff, and Mr. Spanyard making in that direction. Something is likely to happen, Noel."

"He couldn't have recognised them, even through glasses," said Noel. "I think he's friendly."

"Can't chance that now," tersely from Malcolm.

"Something unusual attracted him. Look here, there is no time to waste. I vote we row round to the beach and climb the cliff. There may be trouble. It's up to us to look after Gwen and Dudley," said Noel.

"You mean, leave the Count out of it?" asked Malcolm.

"Suppose he laughs at us?" asked Noel, anxiously. "After all, he might and there isn't a second to be lost."

Malcolm agreed to change of plan. For the first time, the real gravity of the situation was impressed upon their minds, and they were really concerned about the welfare of the two kids.

"We were idiots not to have told Dad, Malcolm."

"It's all my fault," answered Malcolm. "We should not have let the kids go. Come along, let's hurry. I'll row. You take the tiller and keep a sharp look-out. Thank goodness, the oars are muffled."

They ran down the harbour steps and leapt aboard the *Gallant*. No sooner had Noel cast off the painter than

Malcolm pushed the boat away from the harbour wall, and shipped oars.

But for the rippling water off her bows, their progress was silent.

" I'm passing close to the yacht," whispered Noel. " There doesn't seem to be a sign of life aboard."

The water was the colour of a misted mirror, against which the yacht looked ghostly and vague.

It was the silence aboard that puzzled the two boys. Not a sound, not a voice ; not even a light !

She might well have been mistaken for a manless ship !

Their own stealthy, soundless passage, too, was uncanny.

" Rest oars ! " suddenly whispered Noel, throwing the tiller hard over to port so that the *Gallant* drifted away from the yacht that was only a few yards off. " Back water . . . She is just visible from here, but I don't suppose we are to them. Rest on oars."

Noel's eyes were fixed on the yacht.

Malcolm turned his head over his left shoulder, to see what had attracted Noel. He stared.

Beyond the starboard bow, at a distance of about two hundred yards, he saw the white hull. A boat was being lowered. There were six men aboard her. There came a slight splash as she struck water, and a series of leaping ripples expanded and reached the *Gallant*.

The chums crouched low against the gunwale, with their eyes fixed upon the boat. They had heard no orders being given. The running of the falls had been soundless.

The boat from the yacht slipped silently towards the harbour mouth, silently except for the muted rippling and splash of water off her bow.

" Muffled oars and rowlocks," whispered Malcolm. " It looked like the Count in the bow. We'd better get round to the beach. I'm anxious about the kids."

The *Gallant*, being broad of beam, and a weighty keel having been added to counterbalance her spread of sails, required more than meagre muscles to row her for any length of time. Malcolm, however, was sturdy and stronger than most boys of his years, splendidly fit, for boxing and swimming were pursuits in which he indulged frequently.

She was heavy going, despite the motionless waters and no handicapping currents to tax Malcolm's strength to the utmost. The long-boat from the yacht had disappeared.

Leaving the harbour, Noel brought the tiller over to port, and her nose turned. She followed the outer wall of the harbour, shoreward.

As soon as the dusky outline of the cliff was sighted, Noel brought her broadside on to the shore, and made in the direction of Earlie Cove.

Actually, an hour had sped by since they had first seen Mr. Spanyard using night-glasses.

It was an unfortunate whim of fate that Dudley had not remained on the beach ten minutes longer.

Time was not a factor of which Noel and Malcolm were conscious. Their slow progress gave the long-boat an advantage that allowed five of her crew to land twenty-minutes before Noel swung the tiller over and the *Gallant's* keel, a moment later, touched sand.

The solitary man aboard the long-boat was, at that moment, heading out to wait well offshore. They had passed within a hundred yards or so of each other and, had not the chums been intent on watching the coast-line, they would have sighted her vague, whitish passing.

"Drag her up a bit," whispered Noel. "The tide's not quite at the full. Another yard and she'll be safe!"

They heaved, dragging her a few inches at each effort. The noise, as she grated over the sands, was less alarming than it sounded to the chums, who scanned the darkness anxiously.

"It's poss the long-boat landed here," whispered Malcolm. "Anyway, Mr. Spanyard's bunch are on the cliff by now. We've got to reach the door in the wall without being seen, and bring the kids back to the boat."

They ascended to the cliff-top by the same route as Dudley had taken fifteen minutes before.

It was an elongated "V" of tumbled cliff, the point heading inland. Once the height was reached, they crawled. Bushes loomed up, and their progress became very cautious.

Suddenly, Malcolm seized his chum by an arm and pointed ahead, not daring to whisper. There, close to some bushes, was the indistinct outline of a man whom, if he had not moved, Malcolm would have mistaken for a hump of earth.

The two boys suspected the man was stalking a quarry, for he stared fixedly ahead, and moved scarcely an inch at the time. He was prowling rather than crawling.

The chums " froze ", as all scouts are taught to do, pressing their bodies against the ground.

Then, round a farther edge of the bush, that the watcher hugged, appeared another man, who was not aware that he was being spied on, for his face was turned away from the watcher.

It was a tense moment for the two boys.

Suddenly, the watcher rose to a crouching position, and then leapt upon his quarry. The only sound was a stifled gasp and the rapid, heavy breathing of men under great exertion.

The sheer weight of the man who had watched pinioned his quarry to the ground and, before he had a chance to defend himself, three blows to his exposed jaw rendered him unconscious.

Noel touched his chum's arm, and signalled to him to creep into the shelter of the bush.

" It's the Count," whispered Noel, in a trembling voice. " I believe it's Mr. Spanyard he attacked."

Malcolm did not answer.

He peered round the edge of the bush. What he saw was in effect like a shadow-pantomime. Dark against the black bushes, he saw the Count rise. Now there was no mistaking his lean height. Then he stooped, but it was impossible to see what he was doing.

Some minutes later he began to drag his victim towards the slope down to the beach, passing close to the bush that hid the two boys.

They shrank back amid the deepest foliage.

They saw the Count's face clearly as he passed close to them, and recognised Mr. Spanyard! He was being dragged by his bound legs, his head bobbing and dancing over the uneven ground. He was still unconscious.

Motionless, holding their breath, they watched until the darkness engulfed the Count and his victim.

They began to crawl in pursuit. It was an instinctive act. Neither had spoken.

Reaching the cliff, the Count slung the unconscious man across his shoulder, a demonstration of sinew and muscle which neither the boys suspected he possessed.

" If he sees our boat, we're in trouble," breathed Noel.

Fortunately, Count Aland did not make direct for the water's edge. He threaded his way amid the boulders to a point some yards from where the *Gallant* leaned drunkenly to starboard, and dumped Mr. Spanyard on the sands. The chums heard his body thud. They moved to behind a boulder, close to where the Count stood.

Against the heavy greyishness where the tide was thin over the sands, the Count's lean figure loomed like a shadow. He fumbled in several pockets of his jacket, then withdrew a box of matches.

He lighted a match and waved it gently to and fro for a moment or so, the feeble flame tinting his features and sparkling in his eyes, so that they looked like small polished marbles of jet.

Mr. Spanyard twisted his body feebly, and the sound of such slight movements caused Count Aland to turn, and stand threateningly above him.

" Conscious, my friend ? "

" Conscious and by no means finished," faintly from Mr. Spanyard.

" I am by no means finished with you," came Count Aland's cold, mocking voice. " You will join me in a cruise, Mr. Spanyard, or whatever your name is. I have signalled for my long-boat to put in."

Mr. Spanyard made no answer.

" I thought I heard movements close to the bush where I was hidden," remarked the Count. " And a faint sound of a brief scuffle before that. I rather feared it was a trick to draw my men from cover, but they are too well disciplined to act until I give the signal."

" It was no trick. One of your men was caught," admitted Mr. Spanyard, referring to the episode witnessed by Gwen and Dudley. " That was some time ago. You have been patient. But your patience will not help you."

" I have waited a long, long time for this hour, my

friend, and have schemed too carefully to act in haste," the Count sneered. " I came here prepared for surprises. I rather fancied you had a very good reason for idling in Syre."

" Interesting place," snapped Mr. Spanyard.

" *The house* seems to interest those who are strangers here," remarked the Count, ignoring the comment. " Even my young friends, the smugglers, are interested in *the house*. There is something about that house that fascinates. You were watching it tonight."

" Not *the house*, Count. I expected you and your men on the cliff shortly after sunset," answered Mr. Spanyard. " I do not encourage you to hope for success."

" We will be patient, my friend. I win the first round, I think you English say," laughed the Count. " I am most interested to know why you are so interested in me and why you should think I would be on the cliff tonight."

" Information received, Count," answered Mr. Spanyard, coolly. " My concern was aroused. Perhaps you did not suspect that I am the watch-dog of *the house* ? No harm can come of you knowing that now. Once before, there was an attempt to kidnap the boy. It failed. You, the mastermind, hope to succeed this time, but your plans are not so secret as you thought."

At that moment the long-boat from the yacht grated upon the sands. With surprising ease, Count Aland lifted the bound man and carried him to the boat.

" Paprez," the Count addressed the man in the boat,

"see our friend does not escape, and remain here. We shall have another guest soon. Don't be too kind to the prisoner if he becomes restless."

The Count turned and hastened along the beach, leaving his prisoner lying on the stern-sheets of the long-boat, with Paprez guarding him.

Mr. Spanyard did not attempt to move. His brain was still somewhat befogged by the effect of the blow he had received. His bonds were too tight to give him much hope of struggling free, closely watched as he was.

The two boys were astonished by what they had over-heard.

"Mr. Spanyard only tried to keep us out of trouble," whispered Noel. "He said, Malcolm, if ever we wanted a friend . . ."

"I remember."

"I understand now," admitted Noel. "He could not very well tell us the truth, but he knew something was to happen tonight."

Malcolm's face was stern and white : "It's all my beastly fault. I . . . I wanted to show Mr. Spanyard he wasn't smart enough to trick us, and all the time he was our friend. It must have been the Count who spied on us at the cave. I'd like to get even with that beast later. He was using us all the time for his own end."

"There's a chance yet to win through," rather breath-lessly from Noel. "There is only one man in the long-boat. If we could rescue Mr. Spanyard, Malcolm, and steal the long-boat, the Count would not be able to get back to his yacht."

"I'm not so worried about Mr. Spanyard for the moment, as I am over Bertet," whispered Malcolm. "I think the Count hopes to kidnap him. If he succeeds, it will be all my fault. Oh, yes, it will, and it's useless for you to deny that, Noel. I wouldn't believe Mr. Spanyard. And then I wouldn't let you tell your dad when you wanted to."

Well, perhaps if Malcolm had not wanted to be so "big", and prove himself to be a better leader than Bertet Carlsen, they would not have had the perils they went through that night.

"Pick up some decent sized stones, Noel," whispered Malcolm, in a steady voice. "If the worst comes, we can escape in our boat, or hide somewhere until daylight."

Noel held his breath for a moment.

The man in the boat was watching the captive, and his back was towards the shore. At that moment, from the direction of the cliff-top, came shouts and the crackling of bushes as powerful men fought for mastery.

"Come on, Noel, there isn't a second to be lost," warned Malcolm, in a low voice, as he rose. "I believe they're attacking *the house*, but they can't get back to the yacht if we capture their boat!"

Noel said nothing. He picked up a stone. He realised that if they succeeded in escaping in the long boat, and rousing the village, and getting the help of his father, Count Aland would be defeated.

" I only hope the kids have got away with Bertet," whispered Malcolm.

Noel forced a smile, but to him the darkness and the sounds of fighting from the cliff top, were terrifying. He feared that if his brother and sister had failed, and they were found by the Count, they too would be taken aboard the yacht.

He suddenly realised why the bow of the vessel was turned towards the harbour mouth. For a quick get-away !

Noel had no time to think of himself, or to hesitate. He knew every second counted.

Fearlessly, on tip-toe, he approached the long-boat, with Malcolm by his side.

They could see the sailor's broad, powerful shoulders and round head duskily against the dull waters.

CHAPTER XVII

PERIL NOT OVER

DUDLEY, after returning from the beach, found his sister and Bertet Carlsen waiting anxiously for him. He told them he had failed to sight the *Gallant*, and they must make their escape over land.

"Pleese, it dis no good staying here," agreed Bertet. "When it dis light there will be trub-bel surely!"

"There will be trouble any moment, Bertet," said Dudley, grimly. "We must get away quickly."

"It makes one think of all kinds of dreadful things," admitted Gwen. "The darkness frightens me, but we wouldn't dare move if the moon was up."

" There is only one thing to do," suggested Dudley, not aware that he had taken the lead. " I will scout round and see if we can get through. Once we reach the road, there will be a good chance of escaping. You two had better remain here until I return."

" Pleese, it dis for you I feel trub-bel. You leave me and take your dear sister home."

" Oh, nonsense to that," answered Gwen. " That would be a beastly thing to do, Bertet. You can make up your mind we're not going to leave you, so there ! "

Dudley made both promise to remain hidden behind the bush until he returned, unless there was danger, then they were to try to reach Earlie Cove, and wait there until daylight.

" But, if I don't return," Dudley added, in a whisper, " and you are in no danger, remain here until the morning. It will be safe by daylight."

Another long and alarming wait followed for Gwen and Bertet Carlsen.

Gwen now wished she had suggested hiding farther inland, away from the cliff edge. It would have been far better if they had hidden until daybreak.

" Poor Dad and Mum will be in such a state," she whispered, disturbed by the thought of anxiety at home, rather than concerned about her own welfare. " And poor Mrs. Spraggart ! What will she do ? It must be very late and they will all be sitting up, wondering what could have happened to us. And just what has happened

will be the last thing they will think of. Poor dears!
Mrs. Spraggart will be sure we have fallen over the cliff,
and Mother will think we are all drowned. But no one
will think of looking for us here!"

"No harm shall come to you. I protect you with my
life, surely," valiantly from Bertet Carlsen, just as though
he was man enough to stand against several ruthless
ruffians.

At long last, just when Gwen was afraid that something
awful had happened to her young brother, Dudley
returned.

"It's no good trying to reach the wood by going in
front of *the house*," he told them in a breathless whisper.
"There seem to be men all over the cliff. I think they
must be waiting for a signal. We must keep away from
the wall. But we can't remain here."

"Then we must hide, Dudley," Gwen said as bravely
as she was able. "Dad will soon rouse the village, and
have search parties out. We ought to have been home
long ago. Poor Mrs. Spraggart must be in an awful state
of mind."

"She'll fight any man to save us," said Dudley, and
smiled at the thought of what would happen to the Count,
or Mr. Spanyard, if they tried to stop her searching for
her "chicks". "And there are Noel and Malcolm.
Help will soon be coming. But where can we hide,
Gwen? It isn't safe to stay here. Neither would the
beach be any better."

"Pleese, there is the cave," Bertet suggested. "We stay there until day comes."

"But we've got to get there first. It's a bit risky," answered Dudley.

"Of course it's a risk, Dud," agreed Gwen. "But it may be a worse risk staying here. I don't suppose there are any men hidden on the beach. They're going to attack *the house*. They think Bertet is still there!"

Little they knew that, at that very moment, Count Aland was ascending from the beach, having left Mr. Spanyard a prisoner in the long-boat.

"The more we talk, the less we shall do," declared Gwen. "And we must move before the moon begins to rise."

Dudley led the way, crawling inch by inch, making for the beach.

He was no puny, frightened boy now, turning to his sister for aid.

Meanwhile, Noel and Malcolm hesitated on the beach, within a few feet of the long-boat.

The three children had scarcely reached the beach, when commotion broke out from the cliff-top, and it was with a feeling of relief they ran into the shelter of the cave, not a little alarmed by the cries that reached them distantly. Had they taken the opposite direction, on reaching the beach, they would have run into Noel and Malcolm.

"Perhaps Dad and the villagers are looking for us, and Count Aland's sailors!" suggested Dudley.

" It will be safer to remain here until we are quite sure what is happening," warned Gwen.

Meanwhile, the two elder boys were not idle.

" Ready for action ? " whispered Malcolm, as he picked up a stone. " The man is probably armed, and once I get his weapon and free Mr. Spanyard, the Count is defeated."

Their progress towards the long-boat was soundless. The man remained with his back to them, watching his prisoner, and quite indifferent to the voices that still rang out from the cliff-top.

The chums had almost reached the long boat, when Malcolm threw his stone. It was well aimed. The man uttered a cry as he was struck on the side of the head. He had no chance even to move before Noel's stone caught him on the head. He slithered off the thwart, to crash in the bottom of the boat, for a few moments too dazed to know what had happened.

Malcolm leapt the gunwale, and threw himself upon the dazed man, while Noel whipped out his sheath knife and cut the bonds that held Mr. Spanyard powerless.

It was the work of a few breathless minutes before Mr. Spanyard was free. He did not waste precious seconds by thanking them, or asking questions. He turned his attention to the victim of their assault, upon whom Malcolm was seated, disappointed to find that the man was not armed.

" Throw me some ropes," panted Mr. Spanyard, to

Noel. "And be ready to push the boat off if we're rushed. The Count will be back any moment."

The man was quickly bound and gagged. Malcolm rose panting and dishevelled.

"Splendid work!" Mr. Spanyard smiled for the first time. "You're trusting me. No time now for story telling."

"No, there isn't," grimly from Malcolm.

"Good! There is trouble on the cliff-top," said Mr. Spanyard. "My men and the Count's. And you boys keep out of it. Push the boat off, and keep her off shore. Come in if you hear me imitate a gull three times in succession."

Without waiting for an answer, Mr. Spanyard turned to hasten into the darkness.

"Quick's the word," excitedly from Malcolm, as he leapt out and began to push the long-boat into deeper water. "I'll row while you keep an eye on the shore, Noel, and the other eye on that rotter."

The long-boat did not require much of an effort to launch her into deep water. While Malcolm kept her a few yards off shore, Noel watched the prisoner, and shot glances shoreward, in case Mr. Spanyard signalled for their return.

"If that scoundrel bats an eyelid," warned Malcolm, "hit him hard."

"Bet you, I will," promised Noel.

The commotion from the cliff-top had ceased.

"Malcolm, I hope they haven't found the two kids and Bertet," whispered Noel, anxiously. "We ought to have told Mr. Spanyard about them."

"They ought to have got away long ago, Noel."

"I hope so. And Dad is sure to rouse the village as soon as he is back, and hears their story," said Noel, hopefully. "Funny thing, there isn't a light anywhere. Should have thought the row would have attracted the village."

"At the worst, Noel, if the kids have fallen into the hands of the Count, he won't hurt them. Something's gone wrong or he would have returned by now," whispered Malcolm. "I don't suppose the Count can find Bertet."

It was some minutes later before Malcolm spoke again :

"If an attempt is made to rush the boat, Noel, I'm making for the harbour. Once we reach the steps, you dash off and rouse the village, and I'll run home. Your dad will know what to do."

"All right," breathlessly from Noel. "It seems awfully late, and I can't understand why Dad hasn't begun to search by now."

It was very late. They little knew that the car had broken down, and Noel's parents were stranded miles from Syre. It was eleven o'clock, and old Mrs. Spraggart was beginning to get anxious.

"The moon ought to be on the rise just after eleven," said Malcolm. "So it can't be so terribly late, but it seems ages and ages since we left the harbour."

Mrs. Spraggart was becoming more restive with each passing minute. Her "chicks" had not returned to roost, and she made up her mind that this was the last time she would grant a birthday favour. She had no doubt that Master Malcolm was to blame, and, guest or no guest, she intended to give him a piece of her mind.

"I'll give them another half an hour," remarked Mrs. Spraggart, to Mary, the maid. "Master Malcolm will be sent packing if I have my way!"

When the half-hour had passed, old Mrs. Spraggart was more alarmed than angry. She grimly prepared to go in search of her "chicks", rousing the gardener to keep her company. One never knew what might happen to a body in these foreign parts, was her opinion of Syre.

She was becoming frightened, certain that even the headstrong Master Malcolm would not have caused all this trouble. Thank goodness, Mr. and Mrs. Strathmore were not at home.

Armed with an umbrella, hatted and coated as though setting out for the frozen north, old Mrs. Spraggart went down to the harbour, with the gardener. They carried each a lantern.

The darkness and silence filled Mrs. Spraggart with increasing alarm. She hammered on cottage doors, and very soon Syre was astir. The commotion, earlier, from the cliff-top had not reached the village. The folk had gone to bed early, being up with the sun most mornings, and not minded to waste light.

Mrs. " O.H.M.S." Rattle, being a mother herself, offered to lead an expedition to the east cliff, having first made sure that she had hidden " H.M. property " under the wood, butter and behind sundry biscuit tins.

Before the lights shone from many of the cottage windows in Syre, however, and the good people were assembling in some alarm, Count Aland's men had been taken prisoners, at the door in the wall that surrounded the House of Golden Windows.

Mr. Spanyard's men, though less in number, had fought desperately, and won.

The house had been awakened by the sounds of combat, and cries of angry men. Bertet's bodyguard found the tent in the garden empty.

The alarm given, servants and bodyguard searched the grounds, their lanterns twinkling amid the bushes, each armed.

Failing to find the boy in the wilderness of a garden, and discovering that the bolts of the door had been withdrawn, some of the servants came out upon the cliff-top, where they found Mr. Spanyard and his men securing the last prisoner.

The news that the boy was missing surprised Mr. Spanyard. He quickly explained what had happened, and who he was, and why he was there.

He assumed command over the servants.

" Take the prisoners into *the house*," he ordered. " And make sure they do not escape. Harris, Tomlyns, and Warren, rouse the village ! Then, with help, board the yacht and make sure she doesn't escape. The Count has escaped. He may have the boy ! "

He had no time to explain that he feared Bertet Carlsen had joined " the smugglers ", and possibly had fallen into the Count's hands.

Before the villagers could be roused, old Mrs. Spraggart had done so, and Mrs. " O.H.M.S. " Rattle was leading her party to the east cliff.

" Your orders are to search the cliff and shore ! " Mr. Spanyard shouted, as he ran towards the slope down to the beach, anxious for the welfare of the two boys in the long-boat.

Within ten minutes Syre learned, from a messenger Mr. Spanyard had sent, what had happened. A boat-load of fishermen—fortunately all had not gone out on the tide that evening—set off for the yacht, armed with anything suitable on which they could lay a hand.

The yacht was boarded and the guard captured before they realised what was afoot.

Mrs. Spraggart led searchers along the beach, fully minded to give the Count a good biff over the head with her umbrella, before she expressed her opinion of such a wretch, and another for having been greedy at the launching.

The darkness thinned before a rising moon. The shore

was revealed in greater detail to the two boys in the long-boat. Some minutes before the lights appeared in the village, they saw Count Aland running along the shore.

He saw the long-boat and signalled before he realised that it was in charge of two of his " smuggler friends ". He shook his fist in a fine and useless rage, before turning to disappear in the direction of Earlie Cove.

Unseen by the chums, he made a desperate effort to push the *Gallant* into deep water, but her keel had stuck fast in the sands, and he had to abandon the attempt.

Later Mr. Spanyard came racing down the slope, and signalled for the long-boat to be brought in.

" The Count's gone off towards Earlie Cove," shouted Malcolm, as he pulled on the oars.

" Alone ? "

" Yes, sir."

As soon as the keel touched sand, the two boys leapt into the shallow water, and joined Mr. Spanyard. He learned their full story in a few brief statements, but his relief was brief, for Mrs. Spraggart and party appeared.

She sobbed that her " chicks " had not returned, and for no reason at all called Malcolm " a wicked, wicked boy ", and struck him with her umbrella.

" It was you who wanted to play smugglers," she told him, as Malcolm backed away from a second assault.

" You poor, frightened chicks," she cried, the very next moment, and embarrassed Malcolm by hugging him desperately to her bosom. " It's no good talking ! "

" You're right, Mrs. Spraggart," agreed Mr. Spanyard, standing between the old lady and Malcolm, who had wriggled free and was panting for breath. " The Count was alone, thank goodness. The children are somewhere on the cliff-top or making for home."

Old Mrs. Spraggart trotted off towards the cliff-top, a warrior of a woman if ever one existed, commanding the gardener to follow. She kept her umbrella raised, in case some horrid man appeared from cover.

She was followed by a dozen others, including Mrs. " O.H.M.S. " Rattle, who kept on declaring that she had never had such a night. She was armed with a rolling-pin, and was ready to apply it with a vigour ripened by many years of washing and turning the mangle.

The search went on until dawn.

Then, forlorn and anxious, the searchers gathered in the village, where Mr. and Mrs. Strathmore joined them.

Mr. Spanyard proposed that, after rest and food, the search be organised in three parties, and no respite for any until either the missing children were found or darkness made further effort impossible.

CHAPTER XVIII

TREACHEROUS GIFT

SOME were eager to continue the search for the missing children. Mr. Spanyard, however, said that that would be useless until the light improved, and the searchers had had a rest.

The fear was that Count Aland had found them, and that Bertet Carlsen had been kidnapped.

Old Mrs. Spraggart and Mrs. " O.H.M.S." Rattle were against Mr. Spanyard, but he managed to make them realise that a few hours' waiting would make very little difference, and that searching in the dark was useless.

Mrs. " O.H.M.S." Rattle quite expected Count Aland

to rob the post office any moment, in consequence of which she divided her time gossiping with others, and running back to her shop, surprised to find everything in order.

Noel and Malcolm were invited to have breakfast with Mr. Spanyard.

Mrs. Spraggart was persuaded to return home by car, until the search began again, on condition that, should the Count be found, she would be allowed to use her umbrella just once " to show what I think of his airs and graces".

Before boarding the car, Mrs. Spraggart hugged and wept over Noel, then threw her arms around Malcolm's neck, before he could guess her intention.

Malcolm gasped as he struggled to escape, and said that he was very sorry, to which Mrs. Spraggart answered that only a horrid old beast would blame him for wanting to be a smuggler.

Alone with Mr. Spanyard in his cottage, the two boys compelled themselves to eat a breakfast they did not feel like having. Unless " the kids " were found, there was to be no respite in the search until dusk, and not a moment's relaxation. They both realised a good meal was essential, if they were to play their part.

" I ought to have trusted you both," regretted Mr. Spanyard, when they were seated at the table. " But it was not my secret to share. I was paid to watch for strangers coming here. There has always been a fear that your young friend might be kidnapped. Count Aland—that is not his real name—has been looking for him. What did your friend call himself?"

"Bertet Carlsen, sir," answered Noel, rather miserably.

"Ah, well, Bertet was very closely guarded until recently, and then his guard became rather slack," explained Mr. Spanyard. "It was only natural he should want freedom and friends with whom to play. He was fearless, though he knew his life was in danger."

Mr. Spanyard paused to refill their coffee cups.

"Count Aland had a spy aboard his yacht, so I was better informed than he suspected . . ."

"Well, sir," interrupted Noel, "if you knew what to expect, why didn't you warn Bertet?"

"Because, Noel, neither Bertet nor his guard knew me, or why I was here," answered Mr. Spanyard. "I had to keep that a secret. It was a precaution against there being a traitor in *the house*. If I had called in the police, I could have produced no evidence, and Count Aland would have been forewarned. It was my duty to prevent publicity and the newspapers making headlines about *the house*. I was commanded to protect Bertet without revealing to the authorities the danger he was in. I had to act without the help of the law."

"But who were the men you met at Earlie Cove sir?" blurted out Malcolm, without thinking.

"Ah, so my smuggler friend knows more than I

suspect," Mr. Spanyard laughed, surprised but not displeased. "Come, be frank with me and tell your story."

"Well, sir, we saw you down at Earlie Cove last evening," explained Noel, and told the story of the telegram, and what followed.

"And all because I did not trust you," regretted Mr. Spanyard. "But my position was difficult, and events followed much more rapidly than I thought possible. Besides which, you were very friendly towards the Count."

"I can't see why you should have trusted us, sir," admitted Malcolm.

"No reason at all, but knowing what I did and learning you intended to play night smuggling, perhaps I should have seen your father. The Count was using you chaps for his own end."

"The Count was frightfully decent towards us, sir," Noel declared, then added with regret, as he looked through the open doorway at the yacht in the harbour : "We shall never have our trip now."

"I would very much like to know where the Count is," said Mr. Spanyard, thoughtfully. "However, I haven't told you who Bertet Carlsen is, and why his life is in danger. I am telling you in confidence. I am hoping this night's adventure will never get into the newspapers. You have heard of the small European state of Koohn. Perhaps you haven't though. Lots haven't heard of it. It was in the news two years ago..."

"I remember, sir," exclaimed Malcolm. "The king suddenly died, and a dictator usurped the authority of the young prince. He was then at Harrow. I can't remember the name of the dictator, but I remember he was thought to be very brutal."

"Yes, worse than brutal, Malcolm," said Mr. Spanyard. "The old king refused to sell the mineral rights of his country. Koohn is rich in minerals used for munitions, and the king would have nothing to do with war.

"Also, he wanted his people to remain simple and happy, tilling the soil. He knew that if he sold the mineral rights, his subjects would be no richer, but would have to work much harder and less pleasantly in mines controlled by foreigners.

"Well, no sooner was the king dead and the dictator had got power, than the mineral rights were sold. He became very rich, but not the people. He had no right to act like that, and if the prince, young though he is, were to return, the people would fight for him now that they have seen the evil of greed. That is what the dictator is afraid of."

"Why didn't the prince return, sir?" asked Noel.

"Because it was not safe for him to do so. The people were led to believe they would be richer and happier if they left the land and worked in mines," explained Mr. Spanyard. "Now, after two years, they find themselves under the cruelty and greed of foreigners. The time has come for the prince to return, and that is why his life is now in danger. Once he lands, the people will acclaim him. They know how he loves them. And he knows they love him."

" So Bertet is really King of Koohn." Malcolm was deeply impressed. " One afternoon, sir, he told us he wanted to be a king. Of course, he told us nothing about himself but, somehow, as he spoke it didn't sound stupid. If I had talked like that, I would have been laughed at."

" Prince Birheim is only a boy, but he is also a king," continued Mr. Spanyard. " His father was murdered, which the people found out only a few months ago. There was a revolt, cunningly led by the dictator as soon as the king died. It was then dangerous for the prince to return.

" His friends removed him from Harrow. Two trusted ministers, who had fled to England with the Queen Mother, looked after and kept your friend hidden. For two years he has been carefully trained to be king."

" He will be a great king," declared Noel.

" Great kings are those who are good and not necessarily clever," remarked Mr. Spanyard. " He will make a great king. His people are not educated. They are generous-hearted, noble-minded and patient.

" Well, one attempt was made to kidnap Prince Birheim. You remember I told you about a man found unconscious one morning. Somehow, the prince's whereabouts had been discovered."

Mr. Spanyard paused. Already, groups of villagers were gathering in the cobbled street, ready to set out on another search.

" Never mind how I came to learn of Count Aland's intentions here. That is a long story," Mr. Spanyard resumed.

" He is the dictator. He planned to kidnap the young prince, and accuse his enemies of having done so. Perhaps later, when he had influence over the prince, he might have restored him to the throne, and become popular with the people for doing so. I don't know quite what his plans were. There is no doubt, however, that the scoundrel has made wealth out of his treachery, but foreign concessions are not legal."

" Dud believed, from the first, that Bertet was a real prince, and we laughed at him," smiled Noel. " Poor kid, he didn't seem to be afraid last night, though it was dark and we all thought there might be danger."

" Well, we've got to find them. And the Count. He is very clever and cunning," said Mr. Spanyard. " I've no doubt it was the Count who spied on you in the cave. For some reason, he suspected you might have made friends with Prince Birheim."

" I believe he overheard us talking," admitted Malcolm. "That was when we returned to the harbour."

" I remember. You accused me later. I was afraid to say too much in case you repeated it to the Count," explained Mr. Spanyard. " I thought it wiser for the

Count to learn we had quarrelled. I could only hint that it was dangerous for you to play night smugglers."

" Didn't you warn us by a note, sir ? I have it in my pocket. Here it is." Noel produced a screwed-up piece of paper, that had been wrapped round a stone and thrown as they were entering the drive, after their quarrel with Mr. Spanyard. " It was a warning not to play at night smuggling."

" I didn't write that. The Count must have. Obviously, he didn't want you along the cliff last night."

" The point really is," Malcolm said, feeling restored after rest and food, " how did the Count find out Prince Birheim was here ? "

None of them realised then that Gwen and Dudley had innocently said a great deal about their young friend on the previous evening, when the Count had given her the photographs, which he had so generously printed.

" He suspected, of course, but definitely found out after coming here that the prince lived at *the house*," stated Mr. Spanyard. " But my spy on the yacht doesn't know how he found out. I think I can guess. He spied on you that day you went to the cave . . ."

" But we all sat inside the cave, sir, and the boulder in front hid us," protested Malcolm.

" Perhaps so, but I thought I saw Count Aland give you a camera ? "

" Oh, yes sir, he did.   We took some spiffing photographs down at the cave," admitted Noel, and then he frowned as a sudden suspicion swept across his mind. " *The Count offered to print our films !* "

Mr. Spanyard smiled grimly : " A treacherous gift ! It was only boy-like that you should try to find out who lived in *the house*. He hoped you would get to know that boy, and take photographs. His cunning plan was most successful, sooner than he had dared to hope, I have no doubt."

The two boys were speechless from surprise, and both felt angry at such a trick having been played upon them.

" We took snaps," said Noel.

" It was ' a shot in the dark that hit the bull '," regretted Mr. Spanyard. " But neither of you need reproach yourself. I saw him give you the camera and even I—suspecting his evil game—did not realise how treacherous that gift might prove to be."

" I hope Mrs. Spraggart gets hold of him and gives him a good biff with her gamp." Malcolm rubbed his head· " It was a mean, dirty trick, sir."

" Doubtless, Mrs. Spraggart has made up her mind to give the Count a taste of her gamp," grinned Mr. Spanyard. " Now, we're rested and fit again. The light is stronger. What do you boys intend to do ? Mr. Strathmore will lead one party across the cliffs. I'm taking another along the shore, and Harris, and a dozen more, will scout inland."

" There is the cave, sir. I don't suppose they went

there, but Malcolm and I can do no harm by going there," said Noel. " We'll borrow your lantern, sir, and your party can join us later."

None spoke the uppermost thought in his mind. The " kids "—as Malcolm and Noel affectionately referred to the missing Gwen and Dudley—must have met with some accident, otherwise they would have appeared. Indeed, the only hope was that they had gone inland and had lost themselves.

In the cobbled street, the search parties were ready to leave. Mr. Spanyard and the boys joined them. A map of the country was spread on the wall, and consulted.

There was an old ship's cannon in the garden of one of the cottages, which was to be fired as soon as the search proved successful.

The early mists still clung to the valley behind *the house*, and over the sea off-shore.

Mrs. Spraggart appeared on the scene to see them off. She was in such a state of mind that she still wore paper curlers, and flourished her umbrella every time the Count was mentioned.

It was very still.

The House of Golden Windows looked down upon the scene, tinted a warm hue in the light of the rising sun. The good folks of Syre had hated and suspected *the house* from the first. They had never wanted a grand house in their midst, any more than they welcomed strangers, rich or poor. Now the secret of *the house* had drawn them together, in sympathy with strangers in the throes of grief·

Mrs. " O.H.M.S." Rattle had neglected her washing, expressing a hope that " that villain of a Count " would be ducked in her wash-tub later. She attached herself to the beach party, having closed the shop and post office, declaring primly that she was quite sure that " His Majesty" would have no objection, just this once in forty-one years come next firework day.

The parties set out in several directions, watched by the women folk and smaller children.

Noel and Malcolm went ahead of the searchers led by Mr. Spanyard, taking a borrowed lantern and a box of matches.

There would be no joy in Syre that day unless the old ship's cannon thundered over the sea, and sounded off the rugged cliffs in dying, rumbling echoes.

CHAPTER XIX

TRAPPED

"WE shall be safe here," declared Gwen, pausing at the entrance to the cave. "No one would think of looking here for us, and as soon as it is light we can go home."

"That's all very well, Gwen, but there're hours to go before dawn," said Dudley. "Dad and Mum will be in an awful state. We're in no real danger, but Bertet is. And that's the point really. It will be quite safe to go along the beach . . ."

"Oh, no, Dud. At least we're now safe," quite decisively from Gwen. "We'll hide in the cave. It's warm

232

and dry. We can sleep until dawn. Anxiety of Dad and Mum, and the fidgets of poor Mrs. Spraggart, will be better for them than should anything happen to us."

" Pleese, there trub-bel will be surely if you found with me." Bertet was just as anxious on their behalf as they were for him. " It dis better that you leave me."

" Nothing of the kind," firmly from Gwen. " If we stay here talking, someone will hear us and, for goodness' sake, what would happen then ? We'll go a long way into the cave."

Now that real danger seemed to be almost over, and they were comparatively safe, Gwen once again felt responsible for her young brother. Perhaps she was perfectly right in saying that it was better for their parents to spend an anxious night, and dear Mrs. Spraggart " be in a state " until dawn, rather than run unnecessary risks again that night.

" They'll be searching for us long before dawn, Gwen," whispered Dudley, gravely.

" A nice thing if we run out at the first shout and find that horrid Mr. Spanyard," answered Gwen. " We will wait until it is daylight and then we can see what we are doing, Dud. Hold hands. We'll go to where you said the caves branch, then if anyone does come into the cave, we shall be able to run down one branch while they take the other."

They held hands. Gwen led the way, and Dudley came last. Gwen kept her free hand on the roughly hewn wall so that she could feel when they reached the branch.

They thought that the last hour or so—for they had no conception how long the adventure had lasted—had been as black as they thought black could be, but inside the cave the darkness was far more intense and disturbing.

That they were closed in by the cliff, and had only the beach along which to escape, was not a pleasant thought should Mr. Spanyard, or any of those men he met at Earlie Cove, meet them when they hoped to escape later.

Despite the feeling of " shut-in-ness " (which was how Gwen described their cave experience later), both Dudley and his sister felt safe.

Bertet, it would be true to say, knew no fear. If " trub-bel " were to come, he would give a very good account of himself in protecting his friends.

How far Gwen led them into the cave, they could only guess. But it seemed a very long way before Gwen's hand, groping along the wall, suddenly slipped into space, and she knew they had reached the branch.

From a great distance off came the muted echoes of dripping water.

" We had better curl up and try to get a little sleep," whispeerd Gwen (who really was very practical now that she felt they had only to wait for the dawn), and faint echoes of her voice returned, confused and lingering.

Now that they could relax, they felt extremely tired. The stress and strain of their experience had wellnigh exhausted them.

But Bertet fought against sleep, determined to act as watchdog. It was tedious lying there in that darkness, with only the faint echo of dripping water to be heard.

Slowly, his mind was drugged by lagging time.

The next thing he knew was suddenly awakening, his senses acute and suspicious. The night's adventure came back to his mind in a flash.

Very distant was a pin-prick of light, upon which he kept his large, searching eyes.

Gwen and Dudley were sound asleep.

Suddenly, nearer than the pin-prick of light, a weeny flame shot up from the ground, tinting the rugged walls and roof nearby, and revealing a thin face. It was too far off to recognise the person who was seated on the sandy floor of the cave. The glow of a cigarette looked like a lone star.

Bertet realised he had seen a match flame up, and die out. Someone had lighted a cigarette.

Satisfied that his two friends would sleep on, Bertet crawled nearer to the mouth of the cave. Stretched out against the wall, he saw the thin, sallow features of a man against the light beyond the entrance.

Day had come, but they were trapped. Retreat was cut off and to go farther into the cave was dangerous.

Bertet recognised Count Aland, though he knew him to be Baron von Shatzweim, traitor to his father and betrayer of his own people, who had been led to believe their late king had little concern for their welfare, or loyalty towards his country.

But the evil influence of Baron von Shatzweim was already suspected by the people, and the young prince was acutely aware of his own peril at the hands of such a scoundrel.

Worse than personal danger was the peril in which stood his two young friends.

If they were found there now, no mercy would be shown to them. Bertet wondered, if he surrendered, whether the scoundrel would leave the cave, and try to escape with him.

What Bertet did not know was that the Count's plot had failed, and that he was a fugitive in hiding. Any moment, others might enter the cave, which would drive the Count deeper in, to where Gwen and Dudley still slept.

Bertet crawled back to his friends. Placing a hand over Dudley's mouth, he shook him, whispering as the boy stirred : " Not a sound ! "

Then he awoke Gwen, and led them into a branch of the cave.

"Please, your life make not a sound," he scarcely dared to breathe the warning.

Bertet told them of his discovery, and of his fear. They dare not go farther into the cave, and if the Count—as Gwen said—was driven in by a search party, they would be in danger of his evil mood.

" It dis better you not stay with me," Bertet urged. " I will not let him find you surely."

" After all we've been through, we're not leaving you now," insisted Dudley, in a voice that trembled. " I think the Count is hiding, otherwise he would have gone to his yacht. Perhaps they are looking for him now, and if a search party does come, we can shout like billy-ho. He won't have time to touch us."

" Yes, Dud," agreed Gwen, hopefully. " Oh, poor Dad and Mum will be in such a state. We don't want to go deeper into the cave, but nearer the entrance. Then the search party will find us more quickly."

" You're right, Gwen," agreed Dudley. " We may easily become lost. There is nothing we can do except just wait."

Bertet, however, insisted that he should keep ahead of them, close to the Count.

" If he comes farther in, I will give myself up, and then he won't trub-bel about you," he promised, as though that was the easiest thing in the world to do.

" And Gwen must keep behind me," argued Dudley. " Before he has the chance to know we're here, we could take him by surprise. I don't mean now, but when the searchers arrive. Some one is sure to think of the cave ! "

" Pleese, I command you both. If anything should come about . . . Pleese, what do you say ? . . . If anything should . . . happen, you must keep hidden. I go now."

Bertet had given a command in a voice so imperious,

though low, that neither thought of protesting until it was too late, for he had crawled into the darkness, towards the cave-mouth.

" I'm not leaving you, Gwen ! "

Bertet crawled close to the brooding man, his bent figure outlined against the light beyond.

The boy remained hidden in the darkness.

Baron von Shatzweim, alias Count Aland, was a defeated man. The seizure of the long-boat had prevented him from reaching his yacht, and escaping in her.

Several times he went to the cave-mouth, and peered from behind the boulder. He saw the distant harbour and the elegant white hull of his fine yacht rising above the wall. He saw, too, searchers along the beach, some distance off.

Between where he lay and the tide stood Noel and Malcolm. They had paused to light their lantern. Instantly realising they intended to search the cave, his shrewd and evil mind formed a plan.

He was armed, and withdrew his weapon as he hastened back to shelter.

He had little time in which to act.

If those boys entered the cave, he would use them as cover against the other searchers, as hostages. He did not know his yacht had been taken, or he would not have grinned to himself, and had high hopes of escaping.

While he held the boys as hostages, he would demand food and a boat.

He wondered whether the yacht had been taken and, even if so, formed another plan. None would dare to endanger the lives of those boys to prevent his escape.

The plan seemed perfect, and he smiled with fresh hope and certain that he was by no means defeated.

He glanced towards the cave-mouth, and against the strong light saw the two unsuspecting boys enter.

CHAPTER XX

GOLDEN WINDOWS REMAIN

Noel and Malcolm hastened along the beach until they came close to the cave, where they paused to light the lantern borrowed from Mr. Spanyard. Way back, along the beach, search parties were combing the boulders at the foot of the cliff.

The two boys gave no thought as to the Count.

" Those kids must have hidden during the trouble,

and perhaps fell asleep," Malcolm said, hopefully. " I don't suppose they thought of the cave."

" No harm to search there, Malcolm."

Lantern agleam, they paused a few feet within the cave, to accustom their eyes to the increasing gloom.

Count Aland stood rigid behind a projection formed by the sudden widening of the passage, while a few yards behind Bertet Carlsen waited. His heart was pounding as he watched his two friends.

Dudley was too far back from the entrance to see clearly what was happening. Though the gleam of the lantern warned him someone had entered, he had no suspicion it was his brother and Malcolm Brewster.

Gwen, waiting alone in one of the two branches, thought she heard faint voices, just echoes.

Count Aland watched the two boys approach, his smile frigid, his weapon held ready.

Noel carried the lantern above his head, and its light fell upon their faces.

Some yards from the entrance, Malcolm cupped his hands to his mouth and shouted : " Are you here, kids ? "

The echoes of his voice rumbled and died away in a confusion of sound, which frightened Gwen, as the words were indistinct. Her muscles taut, her eyes peering into the darkness, she waited.

Gwen had promised her young brother that she would remain until his return. Now, the waiting was the worst torment of her recent experiences.

Dudley crawled closer to where Bertet was watching.

" Are you here, kids ? " again shouted Malcolm.

Once again, the echoes of his voice died away. His remark to Noel reached Bertet and Dudley quite clearly : " We're fatheads, Noel ! We ought to have examined the sand at the entrance. Can always tell fresh footprints from old. They haven't answered, so it's no good wasting time."

" Oh, well, no harm can come of going farther," answered Noel. " They might not have recognised your voice and are too scared to answer."

He threw the light of the lantern close to the floor of the cave.

" There are all kinds of footprints," he remarked. " Wouldn't think we made so many the other day, Malcolm."

" Half a mo' ! "

It was a sharp exclamation from Malcolm. He snatched the lantern from his chum's grasp, and knelt to examine the sandy floor closely.

" We couldn't have made all these footprints the other day, Noel. And none of us could have made these large ones ! "

Malcolm pointed to several large imprints, that were not confused with a lot of others.

They were close to the projection from behind which Count Aland watched. While they were deeply occupied in studying the footprints, he stepped from cover and cautiously approached the rim of light radiated by the lantern.

" Malcolm ! " Noel's voice sounded alarmingly. " The other day we didn't wear shoes and stockings. Those small imprints must belong to the kids. Both Dud and Gwen wore shoes last night, and perhaps they came here with a man ! "

" What man ? " asked Malcolm, anxiously. " And he limps, Noel. His left foot shows only a faint heel mark."

Malcolm had been taught tracking as a Boy Scout.

Noel's features had gone white : " I . . . I don't think any local kids came here, Malcolm. But why didn't they answer when you shouted ? "

" Perhaps because the echoes scared them," suggested Malcolm. " I say, these . . . these large imprints may belong to the Count ! "

They were silent for a breathless moment.

Noel swung the light around, close to the ground. He stooped and searched eagerly for one clear footprint. Gwen's and Dudley's shoes, like his own, were marked with their initials in nails on the instep. All their boots and shoes were so marked, by regulation of the boarding schools they went to.

Close to the wall, where the sand was firmer and there were very few imprints, he gazed intently upon a footprint

" D. S." was clearly revealed on the instep of the deep, firm imprint.

" Dud's been here, and he wasn't wearing his shoes the other day," Noel whispered. " They're somewhere here, and we've got to find them."

" We'd better fetch help, and more lanterns, Noel," suggested Malcolm, alarmed on behalf of the missing children. " We don't know how many branches there are to the cave and how deep it goes."

At that moment, Count Aland stepped into the light. The chums leapt to their feet, backing against the wall, their eyes riveted on the glistening revolver in his hand.

" Don't move, my smuggler friends ! "

His teeth glistened between his parted lips.

" Just listen to me. Still friends, eh ! So there are others in the cave. We need not worry about them for the time being."

He kept his revolver directed at Noel. Neither of the boys moved nor spoke.

" The life of your young friend is in my hands," he told Malcolm. " Disobey me, and you will regret it. You understand what I mean. Now tell me what has happened."

" Your yacht was boarded and seized last night. There is no escape for you," Malcolm answered. " There are search parties everywhere. The three kids are missing . . ."

" Three ! " exclaimed Count Aland.

Malcolm realised his mistake. He saw an expression

of evil triumph sweep across the Count's features.

"Your young friend from *the house* is with them ! They are somewhere here ! " snapped the Count. " I count myself as being in a fortunate position. Their safety depends on my safety. You must help me to escape."

Noel licked dry lips : " You daren't harm them. They're only children. I'll do anything . . ."

" Ah, that is very wise of you, my young friend," smiled the Count, confident of himself. " We understand each other perfectly. You will remain here, and your friend Malcolm will tell the search parties you have examined the cave. Then your friend Malcolm— remembering your life is in his hands, and so are the lives of the others—will visit the yacht and secretly tell the captain and crew that tonight they must seize the ship and take her a mile off-shore. Your friend Malcolm will help them."

" They are locked in the crew's quarters, under guard," protested Malcolm. " I can't see a way . . ."

" You will ! " sneered the Count. " You must free them. No one would suspect your presence aboard. Before then, return here with food and water. I will look after your friend, and find the others. I will guard them. They will be safe unless you fail, my smuggler friend."

" Don't do it, Malcolm," whispered Noel, desperately. " We . . . we can't betray Bertet."

" You mean, Prince Birheim," corrected the scoundrel,

coolly. "He is perhaps with your brother and sister. You must obey me. Tonight, bring a boat close to here. I promise you, when I am aboard my yacht, your brother and sister will be set free. Now go!"

Malcolm hesitated. He had seen something move behind Count Aland, something vague in the dim reflection of the lantern light.

The next instant Bertet leapt, and flung his arms around the Count's neck.

Sheer surprise, and the boy's weight, unbalanced Count Aland. He reeled a step or so backward, then fell. The revolver went off, the shot ploughing into the roof.

The ear-splitting echo brought Dudley rushing upon the scene, to find Noel and Malcolm fighting the man.

Noel stumbled from a punch that half-winded him, but within an instant he was astride the Count, and Malcolm was seated on his legs.

Dudley saw the revolver on the floor, and snatched it up.

"Move, and I'll shoot!" he yelled, too desperate to realise the nature of his threat.

A brief, fierce tussle followed, during which Malcolm's boot accidentally kicked the Count in the jaw. He was half-dazed by the blow, and incapable of offering resistance.

"Quick, tie his arms and legs," panted Noel. "Use your laces and belts. Anything, but be quick!"

Several moments passed before Count Aland recovered

from the effect of the kick. By then his ankles and wrists were bound. Noel and Malcolm sat on his body, the latter pressing the revolver against the Count's chest. But he kept his finger away from the trigger.

Excited, Dudley ran towards the branch, shouting for Gwen.

" Gwen ! Gwen ! ! Run and fetch help ! ! ! "

" Oh, Dud ! " She threw her arms around his neck. " I heard a shot and . . ."

" No harm done ! Noel and Malcolm are here, and we're as safe as houses," panted Dudley. " Fetch help, and I'll tell you all about it later."

Gwen required no further bidding. Running down the cave, she saw her brother and Malcolm seated on their prisoner, and Bertet holding the lantern. He had a swollen eye.

" Oh, Bertet ! " cried Gwen.

" Pleese, it dis of no harm done surely. They were ver' brave ! "

" You saved the whole kettle of fish, anyway," spoke up Noel. " I say, let's drag him along to the entrance. Gwen, the search parties are along the beach. Shout to them ! "

Gwen ran ahead. She scarcely knew whom she thought had been the bravest.

The old ship's cannon boomed. Its deep roar echoed

off the cliff, and died away far over the sea. Some of the bigger boys were sent racing inland, waving flags to attract the search parties, in case they had not heard the cannon.

Its roar sent the cats flying in panic, the chickens set up a loud cackling, while Syre's three dogs barked themselves dry.

Old Mrs. Spraggart, on hearing the gun, suddenly remembered her hair was still in curlers. Someone offered her a comb, and the dear old soul prepared herself to greet her "chicks". They were returning along the beach with their prisoner, and a number of friends.

No sooner had the gun deafened those down at the harbour, and had broken three windows, than all kinds of wild stories were spread.

Mrs. Spraggart had a vision of seeing her "chicks" return with limbs shot off, an eye missing, and in shreds of clothing.

Mrs. "O.H.M.S." Rattle, returning breathless from the beach, remembered the flags she had put out on VE and VJ Days and, before the party from the cave had reached the harbour, many willing hands had made Syre gay with flags and bunting.

"Oh, you poor dear," exclaimed Mrs. Strathmore, to the fussing and fuming Mrs. Spraggart, who wanted an ambulance, doctors and a whole staff of nurses to be fetched. "They're not hurt in the least. You can see them through these glasses, dear."

"Drat!" Mrs. Spraggart muttered, unable to see anything for her tears.

When the party was close, Mrs. Spraggart was seen to stiffen, and she set her lips very grimly. Her eyes glowered upon Count Aland, and she gripped her umbrella in a manner that boded ill for the scoundrel.

Down the cobbled street and across the cliffs the searchers were returning.

Mrs. Spraggart had an item of stern business to attend to before she "gathered her chicks under her wings", and laughed and cried all over them, after Mr. and Mrs. Strathmore had embraced them.

"You dreadful, awful, hateful old beast!" cried Mrs. Spraggart and, to the protesting yell of the Count, came the rending and breaking of her umbrella across his head.

She felt avenged.

"This is Bertet, Mother," introduced Noel, after the first excitement was over. "He really saved us."

"Pleese," protested Bertet. "It dis nothing surely."

"Prince Birheim, really," impressively from Malcolm.

"Goodness gracious me!" Mrs. Spraggart dropped such a curtsy that a seam gave. "A real live prince and so handsome! How wonderful!"

"Not only a prince," Noel excitedly told his old nurse, in a whisper. "But soon to be a real king!"

Another seam went as Mrs. Spraggart bobbed up and down.

.   .   .   .

The windows of *the house* on the east cliff flashed like sheets of burnished gold. The evening was very still. The flags and bunting hung limp along the cobbled street and down at the harbour.

Noel, his brother, sister and young guests (for Prince Birheim was to stay with them), stood beneath the trees on the edge of the garden-cliff, watching the windows that seemed afire. Now there was nothing mysterious about *the house*, it looked friendly and beautiful.

It was because Dudley had watched its golden windows the first evening on arriving at Syre, that he had wanted to know its story. And the others too !

Its strange influence had drawn them into an adventure that had ended happily.

The House of Golden Windows, when next they arrive for their holidays, will be bright with fresh paint, colourful curtains, and the garden will be gay with flowers, for Prince Birheim will sometimes return there until his education is finished in England.

Maybe, there is a secret yet about the House of Golden Windows, for Dudley believes that when they do explore *the house* they will find a secret passage leading to the cave.

Thus, we leave them standing in silence as the sun flashes upon the windows of *the house*, each thinking that perhaps adventure had begun but not ended at Syre.

When the shadows deepened, old Mrs. Spraggart called her " chicks " and shooed Master Dudley upstairs to the bathroom. He was now allowed to go to bed an hour later than before his birthday.

He had ceased to be a frail, dreamy boy, who had watched the windows of *the house* on the east cliff.

THE END